DON'T OPEN THE DOOR!

Molly twisted the lock and opened the door; she said perplexedly, 'Oh, did you come—?' and then, because of some quality of the silence, her glance dropped to the idly swinging right hand that held the hammer, its head muffled in rags.

She ran. Informed by perhaps the second moment of perfect knowledge in her uncomplicated life, she knew that this had waited for her in the lilac, that she had let it in, that it was now in the house with her and following her with speed and purpose.

She screamed like a child, twice . . .

DON'T OPEN THE DOOR!

Ursula Curtiss

KEYHOLE CRIME
London · Sydney

First published in Great Britain 1969 by
Hodder & Stoughton Ltd

Copyright © 1968 by Ursula Curtiss

Australian copyright 1982

This edition published 1982 by
Keyhole Crime, 15–16 Brook's Mews,
London W1A 1DR

ISBN 0 263 73770 5

Set in 11 on 11½ pt. Times

Photoset by Rowland Phototypesetting Ltd
Bury St Edmunds, Suffolk
Made and printed in Great Britain by
Cox & Wyman Ltd, Reading

CHAPTER
ONE

Even if anybody had believed Molly Pulliam it would have made no real difference in the end. She might have been allowed one more appointment with her hairdresser, or a last afternoon of bridge, or a final fitting of the pink tweed suit she would never wear, but her imminent death was quite a settled thing.

As it was, no one did believe her; not her husband Arthur, nor her sister Jennifer—certainly not the Hathaways, who had been regarding her with a certain reserve ever since. Gradually, a little abashedly, Molly fell in with the general theory of one cocktail too many, the extravagantly high heels she was wearing, a trick of the almost-dusk.

She had been walking home from the Fletchers' cocktail party, a gathering which managed to be both noisy and dull; in addition, she had been on one of her intermittent starvation diets and her two whisky sours were surprising to a stomach lately accustomed to nothing more rakish than carrot strips or a spoonful of cottage cheese. On all counts it seemed desirable to leave. Molly made unobtrusive farewells, refused a ride and let herself out into the end of the late-September day.

It was a bare half mile home along the winding road, but her silky sheath and pumps were not designed for rapid walking. By the time she was nearing her own driveway, marked at one corner by a huge lilac, the sunset dapplings had been swallowed up in dark chiffon light. What a delight it was going to be simply to get unzipped, thought Molly—and the lilac stirred in the utterly still air, and swelled.

In a twinkling, all her senses were engulfed in panic; it was as though some fearful warning had been shrieked at her through the twilight. Involuntarily, knowing only that she must get away from here, Molly began to run.

Her slender high heels and the gravelly road edge betrayed her. In one instant she had her eyes fixed wildly on the lights of the Hathaway house, down and across the road; in the next, she was picking herself up, crying soundlessly, her palms stinging like fire. She had lost one shoe when she fell; she paused fractionally to wrench off the other, with the result that when the Hathaways' door opened under her frantic pounding she was dusty, tear-streaked, and barefoot.

Wizened little Mr Hathaway said in horror, 'Mrs Pulliam!' and then gave a practiced sniff. He suggested warily to Molly that perhaps she had better, er, sit down, and he called his wife.

Mrs Hathaway, a large woman who looked like a block as yet unattacked by a sculptor, had a nose every bit as keen as her husband's. She cast him a significant glance before she said to Molly, 'Has something happened, Mrs Pulliam? Are you all right?'

Molly was still labouring to regain her breath, still weak with reaction at the fact that there were people and lights and a door between her and that terrible swelling in the lilac. She said gaspingly,

'There's someone out there, there's someone hiding in—I was just about to turn in at the driveway and there's no wind at all—'

Drinking, commented the Hathaways' compressed lips and steady inventory of her nyloned toes and dirt-smudged face, but in the end Mr Hathaway volunteered to escort Molly home. He made a preliminary excursion with an enormous flashlight; all it turned up was Molly's pumps.

'I'd have a cup of nice hot soup if I were you,' said Mrs Hathaway in a tone she evidently considered diplomatic as she ushered them out; there was a suggestion that she would spray air-freshener about as soon as Molly Pulliam and her whisky sours had left.

It was now completely dark outside the brilliant scope of the flashlight, but even for Molly the menace in the lilac was gone. It had been there, and it had removed itself. Nevertheless, she was grateful for Mr Hathaway's meticulous room-by-room inspection of the house as she turned on lights and drew curtains and made sure the doors were locked.

Departing he said, 'Will your husband be away for long?'

'No, thank heavens, he's coming home tomorrow.'

'Ah,' said Mr Hathaway profoundly. 'Well, I imagine you'll be all right now, Mrs Pulliam. You probably heard a dog—'

'Dogs aren't tall,' said Molly flatly, and Mr Hathaway, unable to controvert this statement, bowed slightly and took his departure.

Molly went at once to the telephone. Jennifer and her husband, Richard Morley, had often invited her to spend the night when Arthur was away, and their guest room would never be more welcome.

The Morleys' phone did not answer.

They'll be home in a few minutes, thought Molly resolutely, and made preparations for her dinner and changed her clothes and tried the number again, without success. But the feeling of necessity was ebbing fast; the house was securely locked, after all, and whoever had concealed himself so quietly in the dusk had no way of knowing that either she or the Hathaways had not called the Sheriff.

Molly was seldom too shaken to eat. There was cold chicken in the refrigerator, and she made herself a generous sandwich—this hardly seemed the moment for dieting—and presently went to bed. Already dimming in her mind, because she was not an imaginative person, was the inevitability of certain natural equations, like lightning preceding thunder.

Arthur Pulliam came home the next day. He listened to Molly, said, 'Really?' and listened to the Hathaways and said, 'Really!' in a very different tone.

Jennifer Morley, as lean and dark as Molly was rounded and blond, said, 'Face it, you haven't the world's greatest head for liquor, and the Fletchers' parties would send anybody around the bend. Granted there was somebody behind the lilac, don't you think it was boys, just out after mischief, and they got scared off? Remember the robbery the Armstrongs had, and that was in broad daylight.'

Boys. Seeing the carport vacant and the windows dark, assuming that the house would be empty for the evening, starting guiltily in the hollow-centred old lilac so that it had changed its shape in that frightful way . . . It was a reasonable and even a graceful explanation, and because Molly was optimistic by nature and usually held the convictions of the person she had talked to last, she accepted it.

She was not even faintly nervous on the evening of October tenth.

'Going to be all on your own tonight, hon?' Iris Saxon folded the last of the beautiful weekly ironing and gave Molly a fond and roguish wink, startlingly girlish in her severe, wrinkle-netted face. 'Don't do anything I wouldn't do.'

'Well, with me you never know,' said Molly in the same tone, and Iris laughed, cocked her head at the sound of a car in the drive, said, 'There's Ned. See you next week,' and let herself out.

Molly was guiltily relieved that Iris's husband had not had time to come to the door for her. For some reason she had a sense of acute embarrassment with Ned Saxon, perhaps bound up in the fact that, out of work himself, he was collecting his gentle elderly wife from her job. Ned, possibly aware of this, seemed to enjoy pinning Molly down relentlessly on subjects she knew next to nothing about, with the result that she had to listen helplessly while he reconstructed foreign policy or told her what the junior senator was really up to with that farm bill. These sessions were frequently conducted in the windy open doorway while Molly's hair spun in her eyes, or it was well below freezing and she was clutching a sweater about her.

But tonight that had been avoided. Although

Molly would not have admitted it, she rather enjoyed Arthur's absences from home. She had her bath early then, changing into a housecoat and slippers, and ate what she pleased for dinner while she watched something unimproving on television. After dinner she could stack the few dishes in the dishwasher, arrange the pillows in the bedroom and read until three in the morning if she felt like it without disturbing a soul.

By the time she had had her bath, on this evening, the windows were dark. Unlike many women in a house fairly well isolated in its own grounds, Molly was not nervous alone at night. She did the obvious things, like locking the doors and drawing the curtains, but she did not people the closets with faceless assailants or imagine the faint creak of tree branches to be some stealthy approach from outside.

She had put on spareribs to simmer—something both Arthur and Jennifer would have disapproved heartily—and poured herself a small glass of sherry when the telephone rang.

'Hi,' said Jennifer's crisp energetic voice. 'How would you feel about being picked up for dinner now that Richard's been called out to show a house and we're both left flat?'

'Oh, I'm in my robe and I've got things started here. I don't think—'

'Unstart them,' said Jennifer with the unconscious authority of being five years older. She added alluringly, 'I've got lobster.'

Molly hesitated, and the bubbling spareribs, which had now been joined by sauerkraut, sent out an enticing whiff. All that remained was to make dumplings. She said, 'Thanks Jen, but I'd really rather stay in,' and lightly, carelessly set the time of her own death.

There was a swishy wind around the house, a cold autumny sound which made the lamplight and tranquil pretty living room that much more attractive. Molly finished her sherry, watched a panel show which Arthur would have denounced with an angry rattling of his newspaper, and was beating the dumplings when there was a knock at the back door.

Molly paused in surprise, chattered the spoon against the edge of the mixing bowl, and opened the door that led into the small utility room. She was not foolish in spite of her sunny confidence; she switched on the outside light for a look at this unheralded visitor before she went to the back door itself.

Radiance showered down on the familiar creamy-orange head. Molly twisted the lock at once and opened the door; she said perplexedly, 'Oh, did you come—?' and then, because of some quality of the silence, her glance dropped to the idly swinging right hand that held the hammer, its head muffled in rags.

She ran. Informed by perhaps the second moment of perfect knowledge in her uncomplicated life, she knew that this had waited for her in the lilac, that she had let it in, that it was now in the house with her and following her with speed and purpose.

She screamed like a child, twice.

CHAPTER
TWO

The brutal and apparently senseless murder of Molly Pulliam rocked the quiet Valley. Unlike the occasional stabbing in a bar in downtown Albuquerque, or the predawn bullets with which estranged husbands and wives estranged each other permanently, this came close in every respect. It had an appallingly cosy, this-could-happen-to-you atmosphere.

The very domesticity of the setting was shocking. People who dealt in drugs, or regularly gave all-night parties, were never far removed from the risk of violence—but here there were spareribs and sauerkraut burning on the stove while dumpling batter waited in a mixing bowl. Again, multiple divorcees often had multiple enemies among both sexes, but this victim was a cheerful pretty wife of fifteen years' standing.

Moreover, Molly Pulliam, alone in the attractive adobe house, had not been the only vulnerable target in the area on that particular night. Not a mile away Vera Paget was also watching television while her psychiatrist husband spoke at a banquet at a downtown hotel; within the same radius elderly Mrs Heinemann knitted drowsily while baby-sitting for her son and daughter-in-law. Both carports were empty, both homes would have looked equally promising to a burglar.

That the original intention had been robbery

seemed inescapable. There was the smashed pane in the back door, the sound probably covered by the television programme in progress in the living room, through which the intruder had only to stretch his hand and twist the lock. There was Molly Pulliam's emptied pocketbook, the small possessions scattered on the floor and the wallet missing. Molly Pulliam herself lay face-down in the doorway between kitchen and dining room, in a convulsive position although the first terrible blow to the back of her head must have killed her. There had been successive blows.

Although Richard Morley, the dead woman's brother-in-law, had apparently used his head when he arrived on the scene at a roughly estimated hour after the murder—he had turned off the gas under the reeking dinner but touched nothing else—the case had an air of failure from the start. The autopsy declared the weapon to have been a hammer or other implement with a circular edge, wielded with extreme force, but no weapon was found. Fingerprinting was done, routinely and unrewardingly. Footprints were never even a hope: there had been no precipitation for six weeks and the ground was wind-scoured almost to the consistency of stone.

Jennifer Morley, eyes burning and voice ragged as she fought the sedatives she had been given, told them of her sister's recent experience and there was a brief spurt of interest in the huge old lilac. Inspected minutely, it yielded a cracked pink plastic spoon, a few ancient scraps of paper, and the mummified skin of half an orange. Nevertheless, Sheriff's officers dutifully questioned the Hathaways, who agreed that Mrs Pulliam had certainly seemed very frightened but had been—here their glances dropped repressively while their eyebrows went up—'tired and not really herself' at the time.

'What I don't see is *why,*' Jennifer kept saying to Richard, to Arthur Pulliam, to the investigating officers. 'Molly would have been frightened to death of a burglar, she wouldn't have resisted him for a minute. She'd have handed over her purse and anything else he asked for, like—like bank tellers and people in stores when there's a holdup. Why did he have to kill her?'

Panic, the deputy told her. Prepared for a burglar, Molly Pulliam might have acted as sensibly as her sister thought; coming without warning on a stranger who had forced his way into her home at night, she had much more probably screamed and run, triggering an answering panic and a wild violence in the intruder. The deputy did not add that this argued an amateur criminal, which would make him that much harder to find.

Nor was he aware, because he knew the Morleys only by sight from his routine patrols of the Valley, of the strange gulf between husband and wife. He saw the comforting grip of Richard Morley's hand on his wife's shoulder and could not know that her muscles had stiffened; he saw her wan upturned smile and could not know how it made her mouth ache.

Because Jennifer would not put it into words. Although she and Molly had been closer than many sisters, she had turned, after the first incredulous grief, into a woman operating by remote control. In spite of her basic dislike of Arthur Pulliam she had insisted that he stay with them through the first

forty-eight hours of shock, and she had been attentive to his diet. She was calm even through the
massive descent of Arthur's relatives from Wichita,
all of them breathing camphor and disapproval
from every pore. All other members of the family,
their manner made clear, died in hospitals and had
the best of attention before the end.

Jennifer, already rubbed too raw for any reaction
as strong as amazement, realised with dim wonder
that Arthur was absorbing some of this; mingled
with his grief there was now an air of petulance. 'I
really don't think,' he observed to the company at
large, 'that the newspapers need have made so
much of the—details of the dinner preparations.'

Bald male and frizzled female Pulliam heads
moved ponderously in assent. 'A little pheasant
and some fresh asparagus would certainly have
looked nicer,' remarked Jennifer, dangerously
quiet as she rose and left the room, but that was the
only liberty she allowed her stretched nerves.

When Richard, following her into the kitchen,
said in a low voice, 'Jen, for God's sake! I know you
keep thinking—' she raised her eyebrows politely at
him. 'What I keep thinking is that all those—
people, would you call them?—have planes and
trains to catch very soon, so if you'd give me a hand
with this coffee . . .'

She refused, steadfastly, to discuss a period on the
evening of Molly's death. After her own solitary
dinner she had settled down to work on the beige
cable-stitched sweater she was knitting for
Richard's birthday. She reached the armholes,
counted stitches perplexedly, and went in search of
her instruction book before remembering that she
had lent it to Molly.

At once the sweater assumed an imperative nature, although Richard's birthday was still four weeks off, and knitting seemed the only possible way to pass the time until he got home. When Molly's telephone did not answer, Jennifer thought idly, She's in the tub. She made herself a second cup of coffee and tried again, and was hanging up, frowning, when Richard arrived.

He looked tired and irritable. There must, he said, be a special corner of hell reserved for people who made an appointment with a real estate broker—an evening appointment at that—and then failed to show up.

Jennifer sympathised, somewhat absently. She dialled the Pulliam number once more, waited, and put back the receiver; her frown had deepened. 'I wonder where in the world Molly is? Richard, if I make fresh coffee while you're gone, would you just drive over and check?'

Richard expostulated. He had just climbed out of his car; he was tired after the day, the dinner that had consisted of a snatched hamburger, the futile vigil in that damned empty house. Molly was a grown woman who might have a dozen good reasons for not answering the phone at the moment; just what was Jennifer imagining could have happened to her?

His brisk impatience ought to have made Jennifer feel foolish, but it did not. She wasn't so much worried as baffled and annoyed at the total strangeness of the situation, and she said crisply, 'Well, I'll go, then, but you'll have to give me your keys. I've just remembered that I'm almost out of gas.'

Richard gave her a wry look—they had both

known all along that he would go—and poured and drank a cup of coffee with perverse deliberation before he departed.

How many minutes lost there? Had a gloved hand been reaching in for the back door lock, had Molly been screaming with terror while they stood and debated in their kitchen? Logic would presently tell her no, but after only three days logic had a very small voice indeed . . .

While the Sheriff's officers questioned known robbery-with-violence offenders, the frightened Valley took its own steps. Although in this country most householders owned a gun and most wives knew how to handle it, the three local hardware stores quickly ran out of heavy bolts and chains, and the animal shelter was emptied of its large-dog population. Children ordinarily allowed to roam were planted sternly before television sets; instantly they developed a hatred of television, fraying their mothers' nerves to the point where all door-to-door salesmen and innocent meter-readers were reported to the Sheriff's office as, 'There was something very suspicious about that man, Officer. I think it was his eyes. You could tell he wasn't normal.'

There was certainly no reason for anyone to question a very small boy at 159 Allendale Road, and it would not have helped them if they had.

CHAPTER THREE

'I think,' said Iris Saxon, glancing up from the ironing board in Eve Quinn's small kitchen, 'that the little boy is doing something to your chrysanthemums.'

Eve put down the letter she was reading and stifled a sigh. Although her young cousin Ambrose had been visiting her for three weeks now, Mrs Saxon still referred to him implacably as the little boy and followed all his activities with a distinctly chilly eye. Eve found this somehow surprising in the older woman. Ambrose was spoiled, certainly, but so spoiled as to be almost laughable; every time he opened his mouth he posed a challenge.

All that was visible of him when Eve crossed the shadowed grass was one arm and his sneakered feet; the rest of him was engulfed in an enormous conical straw hat someone had brought Eve from Bermuda. Squatting absorbedly, crooning to himself, Ambrose was daintily bringing a chrysanthemum down to ground level with a pair of manicure scissors.

'Reeds,' he said in his sweet precise voice as Eve took away the scissors.

'They're not weeds, they're flowers.' Would it be advisable to show him some real weeds, and let him—? No. 'I wish you wouldn't wear that hat,' said Eve.

Ambrose settled the hat firmly over his

shoulders, and, head back so far that the fringe fell only to his nostrils, gazed combatively up at her through the mild October light. 'I get sunburn,' he said.

Perhaps because he was an only and much-cosseted child, Ambrose had for his own person the deep reverence of a patriot for the flag. His shrieks at the smallest injury were of genuine horror, and at the end of every day he examined his collection of scratches and mosquito bites much more lovingly and anxiously than any mother could have done. He was kind enough to confide his findings to Eve— or at least she supposed he did; although his enunciation was that of a grammarian he made up some very odd words.

He was now blinking his long pale blue eyes at her from behind the disconcerting wisps of straw. 'Saxon took my rockles,' he announced.

'*Mrs* Saxon,' corrected Eve hastily. Too late, she realised that this implied agreement, although she had no idea of what Ambrose's rockles might be. For that matter, Mrs Saxon, who shared her husband's all-embracing fears of catastrophe and had no grasp of the immense deference in which Ambrose held himself, did take a great many things away from him; she seemed to have a belief that small boys should be neat, clean, silent, and totally safe at all times.

'Mississaxon,' sang Ambrose trippingly and, liking the sound of it, raised his voice and tried it a few more times. From the corner of her eye, as she shushed him, Eve caught the sharp turn of Iris's head behind the kitchen window and knew, in an instant of discernment, where the friction lay. Philadelphia-bred, used to considerable material

comfort until her marriage and the long slow progress to desperate poverty—Eve knew this from
Jennifer Morley, the wife of the real estate broker
who had found her this house—Mrs Saxon could be
casual and humorous while doing domestic work
for the first time in her life in the society of her
peers. It was the presence of an odd and noticing
child like Ambrose that made her feel betrayed and
demeaned.

The conical hat slipped forward, obscuring
Ambrose to the waist. Emerging from it, turning a
deep executive red, he shouted, 'I want my
rockles!' and partly to mollify him, partly because
she felt awkward in the face of Iris Saxon's grief
over the dead Mrs Pulliam and would just as soon
not go back into the house just yet, Eve submitted
her hand to his imperious tug.

Her own reflection in a window caught her briefly
by surprise: a fair-haired girl whose face was perhaps too thin, companioned by an animated hat.
For just an instant the child, the grass, the little
adobe house swam together in a dizzying reversal of
the this-has-happened-before feeling. The background of six months ago was the real and solid one,
and this some strange projection of the mind . . .

She was living, this other Eve Quinn, in an apartment in a glass-and-concrete structure which
glowed with pride at being all of six storeys high
She was a copywriter with the advertising firm of
Cox-Ivanhoe, and she was engaged, except for the
ring, to William Harper Cox, who had been trans-
ferred from the Chicago office.

It had been a rapid courtship, and it should not
have come as a jolt to Eve when, along with the

ring, came William Harper Cox's insistence on a wedding in the almost-immediate future. He was more businesslike than ardent about it; his manner said, 'All right, we've had the preliminaries, now let's get on with it.' Eve began to feel a little like a piece of necessary furniture for which, if he could not have delivery at once, the impatient would-be buyer would shop elsewhere.

Inevitably, because Bill was not a good dissembler, it emerged that he had been promised a vice-presidency in the firm by his uncle, the ruling Cox, only when he gave evidence of having 'settled down'; in his case, this implied the married state. Eve knew that he was certainly very attracted to her, possibly even in love with her. It was also possible that as a husband he would be as steady as a rock, and that they would both be able to dismiss and forget forever this underlying factor in their marriage.

Someone else might have managed it. Punctiliously, and to the obviously genuine regret and embarrassment of old Mr Cox, Eve resigned from the agency. She reflected, as she cleaned out her desk and found a favourite compact for which she had been conducting periodic hunts in her apartment, that the curiosity of the rest of the copy department about the dissolving of this happy and handsome match was almost pitiable. The secretaries, it was clear, were thinking in terms of some vengeful female turning up on Eve's doorstep, complete with waif.

Was the truth better, or very slightly worse?

The mood of detachment did not last; she quickly discovered the very sound basis in reason for the trips abroad taken by broken-hearted young women of another day. She was not broken-hearted, but she felt almost physically damaged from head to foot—perhaps because that was where pride lay, she thought ironically—and she was in violent rebellion against the surroundings and the friends who had been the witnesses of her naïve and tranquil happiness. Her perusal of the real estate columns and eventual contact with Richard Morley, who found her the house in the Valley, dropped her into another world.

It was a rented house on a cottonwood-shadowed corner, surrounded by an adobe wall and big enough only for a single person who liked elbow room or a childless married couple. Single people usually preferred apartments and wives felt strongly about built-in kitchens and closet space, neither of which was a strong point of the house. But it had a step-down living room with a curved corner fireplace and one whole wall of bookshelves, and its windows were set so low that an apricot and a plum tree and wildly neglected grass seemed part of the interior. Eve took it at once.

Somewhat to the mystification of Richard Morley, she was uncomplaining about the dilapidated state of the house; she wanted to be fiercely busy, and she was. With the help of Iris Saxon, whom Jennifer Morley enlisted on her behalf, she got the tall windows curtained, the kitchen shelves papered, the brick floors clean and shining.

On an evening when everything had been done, and lamplight touched the cool white walls and folds of blue toile in the living room, Eve was seized by something close to panic. She had been in the middle of writing a résumé which she would send to the other advertising agencies in the city; she ripped the sheet out of the typewriter and wrote instead to her first cousin Celia Farley in New York, inviting her and her son Ambrose to come out for a visit.

She and Celia had grown up together, and were more like sisters than cousins. Eve had never met Roger Farley, but knew from Celia's sporadic letters that he was just finding his feet in a brokerage house and couldn't take any time away. But Celia, and Ambrose . . . ?

Celia was delighted. They came, and Eve moved into the tiny space which had to serve as a guest bedroom. By day she drove them up on the mesas, to Santa Fe, to nearby pueblos; by night, with Ambrose asleep, they caught up the threads of distant relatives remembered only from long-ago weddings and funerals.

'Does anybody know what happened to Eugene?'

'Yes, he finally married that girl with all the teeth and the mountains of hair.'

'And the Kerrigans' uncle—was it Patrick?'

Celia rolled her eyes upward. 'There's a bounty on the head of whoever finds him.'

They had been there two weeks when Celia, on the diving board at the local indoor pool, called, 'I wonder if I can still do this?' and tried to execute a double back flip and broke her back.

The confusion at the pool, with Ambrose screaming distractedly; the long-distance call to Roger, his distraught arrival and understandable glance of ferocity at Eve, the indirect author of this crisis: all Eve remembered of it very clearly was standing in the hospital corridor and saying to Roger, 'I know you want Celia back in New York with her own doctor, but I'd be glad to keep Ambrose out here with me until things get straightened out a little.'

She knew that a considerable amount of money, or some rallying relatives, might have taken care of the situation. Celia and Roger did not have the money, and Roger's mother, who lived with them in the apartment on Sixty-first Street, was in a wheelchair. And if Eve had not invited Celia to Albuquerque, had not taken her to the swimming pool . . .

. . . Ambrose stayed.

With all this dashed briefly against her consciousness and then falling away like water from glass, Eve realised that Ambrose had halted and was pointing at the weathered tool shed at the very back of the circumscribed grounds. 'Rockles,' he said expectantly, and then greater volume, 'I want my rockles.'

In the same firm tone Eve answered, 'Well, that's one place they aren't, Ambrose.'

He could not possibly have wandered into the tool shed; Eve had seen to that by attaching a padlock because of the sickle and other tools there, the moist cobwebby darkness with its possibilities of spiders or worse. Eve was not too far away from her own childhood to realise that for lack of a contemporary to say, 'I dare you,' Ambrose might well say, 'I dare me,' out of a combination of swagger and deep fright. Certainly, having dragged her so insistently to the tool shed, he had a curiously riveted stance. He wanted his mysterious treasure, but he wanted Eve to get it.

She had her own distaste for the shed; on her last

visit there, in search of grass clippers, a furry black spider had leaped nimbly onto her wrist. She said with great firmness, 'You can't possibly have left anything in there, Ambrose. Come on, it's almost time for your bath . . .'

It seemed odd, looking back, that no chill invaded the innocent, bird-twittery sunlight, and that the usually indeflectable Ambrose simply rammed the hat down farther over his person and said no more on the subject.

With the night came the wind; it was going to be an early autumn. In the house that had been tramped through and photographed and stared at by avid sightseers, Arthur Pulliam, managing to look like a photograph from an old album even in his pyjamas, lay in bed and gazed at the ceiling. He did not part his hair in the middle or wear steel-rimmed glasses, but he gave that impression. His thoughts were very much his own.

A few miles away, Richard Morley had also gone to bed, after saying gently and unavailingly to his wife, 'It's getting late, you're tired . . .' Jennifer Morley shook her head and went on regarding her book without seeing it. When the bedroom door had remained closed for fifteen minutes she went quietly to the telephone; her implacable, untouchable politeness had been replaced by a look of tense concentration. She dialed. She said very softly, 'Mr Conlon? Is this by any chance the Henry Conlon . . . ?'

Eve Quinn and Ambrose were fast asleep, Ambrose having been deprived of the monstrous hat in which he had retired and been discovered by Eve scarlet and heavily bedewed. It lay beside him on his pillow, a long neatly folded triangle with a dripping fringe.

On a very different kind of pillow, in the county jail, and oblivious from an entirely different cause, reposed a man whom the patient combings into the murder of Molly Pulliam had turned up: a yardman who had worked for the Pulliams several months ago and been discharged for theft. He had been heard to mutter vengefully. He was presently in a state of drunkenness dangerously akin to coma.

The Saxons were preparing for bed, having been made late by having to cash Eve Quinn's cheque and being caught in a long line at the supermarket where they shopped. The wind seemed viciously loud around their small apartment with its occasional startling incongruity; a beautiful old lace cloth which had belonged to Iris's mother dipping its fragility over a scarred formica table; a small painted figurine bought on a trip to Italy.

Iris Saxon was braiding her hair; Ned, of necessity only a few feet away, was polishing glasses with a fanatical eye, holding them up to the bare ceiling bulb, polishing them again. He stopped suddenly and listened. 'What's that?'

A year ago, Iris Saxon would have said tranquilly, 'Oh, the wind.' Now she listened as tensely as her husband. There was a rustle of leaves outside, the progress of a dog to other ears, but Ned Saxon instantly darkened the light, and moving swiftly for so bulky a man, snatched up a heavy flashlight and let himself softly out into the night.

A drug ring, Iris had come to believe. Silent and terrible strangers who used the path beside their apartment to convey marijuana or worse to the people who lived across the street, the people who came and went at all hours and often woke the Saxons out of their much-needed sleep. A small voice deep in Iris's memory remarked that there could be other and innocent reasons for such behaviour, but it was easily stilled.

Ned Saxon came in, breathing heavily and angrily. 'Got away again, darn it. I'll rig up a trip wire out there tomorrow, and then we'll see how slippery they are.' He gazed anxiously at Iris, now in bed, her long greying braids surprisingly childish on the pillow. 'Tired?'

'Not really . . . it's been such a shock about poor Molly. You know, I can still hardly believe it.'

'It was a shock all right,' said Ned soberly. 'You remember, when you first started going there, how I warned Arthur Pulliam that he ought to keep a big dog around a place like that? Asking for a robbery, in that neighbourhood, but of course he knew best . . .'

Iris had drifted off to sleep. Ned pulled the blankets protectively close about her and went to bed himself. The last lamp, just before he switched it off, shone on his creamy-orange head.

CHAPTER
FOUR

A headline in the morning paper said, 'Pulliam Slaying Suspect Found Dead in Cell.' An autopsy had been ordered to determine the cause of death.

In the course of a year, a surprising number of inebriated prisoners did not survive the night. Whether they might have succumbed as speedily if they had been allowed to lie in the doorways and alleys where they had been picked up, it was impossible to know. But with the passing of Silverio Baca, forty-five, the Valley heaved a cautious sigh of relief.

He suited everybody so nicely. There was his grievance against the Pulliams, his familiarity with the house and grounds, a past conviction for burglary. When apprehended in a small unwholesome bar he had been in possession of twenty dollars, an odd fact in itself as he was currently jobless, and although he was far too drunk to make any attempt to account for his whereabouts on the night of Molly Pulliam's death he had resisted the arresting officer so violently that he had had to be, in the demure terminology of the report, 'subdued'. This violence might have been simply distaste for being bundled off to jail; equally, it might have sprung from fear.

In any case he was dead, either from acute alcoholism or injuries suffered from a theoretical fall in his cell, and there was the unmistakable air of a life for a life—his for Molly Pulliam's. 'Save the expense of a trial,' said some people grimly, and other voices added, 'Even if he'd been convicted he'd have been out again in a year, able to do it again.' Easily dismissable, perhaps because the newspapers had garbled the account and used conflicting home addresses, was Silverio Baca's widow's claim that the twenty dollars had been in payment of a debt, and that her husband had spent the evening in question at home.

Jennifer Morley accepted the premise of Baca's guilt with fierce unthinking anger. Arthur Pulliam accorded it more measured consideration. 'To think,' he said, his neat old-fashioned face stiff with outrage, 'that I once gave that fellow an old suit and overcoat of mine.'

To Iris Saxon, who had had only an occasional distant glimpse of the man as he tied up roses or cut the Pulliams' lawn, the case seemed automatically solved. She was astonished when her husband folded the newspaper and commented, 'Very nice and neat for the police, isn't it?'

Iris making peanut-butter and jam sandwiches for their lunch, put the knife down and stared. 'You mean you think he didn't do it?'

'I mean it all seems very providential,' said Ned, pacing importantly. In spite of his bulk and his sixty years, his clear blue eyes and the curiously deepened colour of his hair were uncannily reminding of the slender impetuous young man who had captivated Iris Dickinson so long ago; of his odd patterns of thought there was no physical trace. In this he resembled his wife: she often seemed like a little girl trapped unwittingly in a net of wrinkles and grey hairs.

'The Sheriff's office really bore down on this thing, because Arthur Pulliam is an important man in a way and pays a lot of taxes.' Ned Saxon said it with an air of thoughtful gravity. 'They must have gotten a list of possible suspects from Pulliam right away, and how many people had he fired lately? But it's three days before they catch up with this Baca, and then he's too drunk to make sense or talk back at all, and then he's dead. He was a scoundrel, no question about it, but,' said Ned in a distant and brooding tone, 'I just wonder . . .'

The wonder was very little shared. The investigation into the death of Molly Pulliam could not be officially closed, but the taut vigilance relaxed a little. Bolts and chains were still fastened securely at night, but a few large dogs, one of which had gratuitously bitten its new mistress, were returned to the animal shelter. A door-to-door salesman sold two vacuum cleaners in the area, and previously captive children were allowed to stay out until dusk. This alone had a tranquilising effect on everyone's nerves.

Like people shocked by an earthquake in a part of the world where there are not supposed to be earthquakes, the Valley residents began putting things back together, not suspecting that there would be another tremor, quite soon.

Arthur Pulliam was so badly frightened by the sound of his front-door chimes that he froze momentarily against a wall, thinking with unaccustomed wildness that he would not answer, that he would wait until he heard the further sounds of retreat. Then common sense suggested that this could hardly be the visitor he dreaded—not this soon, and certainly not in broad daylight. Moreover, there were two people; straining, he could hear a murmured interchange.

When he opened the door the Saxons stood there, and while Arthur would normally not have been pleased to see them—he would have preferred to say what he had to say by telephone—his relief was so great that he was almost cordial as he asked them in.

'We just stopped by for a minute,' said Iris, crisp and distinct, 'because Ned wants to fix that bracket that he promised M—that he didn't get around to last week—'

'Oh, don't bother about that,' began Arthur, but Iris continued firmly, '—and there are a few things of mine that I'd like to pick up, because of course you won't be needing me any more.'

Thus anticipated, Arthur was very faintly put out. He had never been at ease with Mrs Saxon, largely because it was impossible to treat her as a regulation employee. Neither Molly nor Jennifer, he knew, had ever issued any orders; when there was something out of the usual routine to be done, it was always, 'Iris, would it be a terrible nuisance . . .' or, 'If you get a chance . . .'

Such a state of affairs was distasteful to Arthur, who liked people who worked for him to be very much aware of the fact. Mrs Saxon had never shown him anything but a courteous mixture of friendliness and civility, but it would have been as unthinkable to rebuke her, if the occasion arose, as it would be to slap one of his aunts.

He had therefore rehearsed a little telephone

speech in which he would thank her gravely for past
services, assure her that Molly had valued her
acquaintance, and explain that in his tragically
altered circumstances . . . and so forth. Although
he was genuinely regretful about the loss to the
Saxons of that small but much-needed weekly income, he would rather have enjoyed it—and here
was Mrs Saxon murmuring politely, 'Excuse me,' as
she walked past him, while from the kitchen came
the sound of hammering.

Arthur was on somewhat firmer footing with Ned
Saxon, even though the older man steadfastly
refused payment for the small repairs he effected in
the homes where his wife worked. He would
present the bill from the hardware store, go over it
meticulously, and accept no more than that even if
he had made special trips in his car; there was a
strong suggestion that any such repairs had been
made for his wife's comfort and safety.

He was now reinforcing a bracket under the
shelf, over a long sweep of formica counters and
steel sinks, which held Molly's cherished collection
of pewter. 'That's very kind of you,' said Arthur,
and added perfunctorily, 'Perhaps you'll have
something to drink?'

In three simultaneous responses, Ned Saxon laid
down his hammer and said consideringly, 'Well,
now . . .'; Iris Saxon said briskly from the other end
of the kitchen, 'Thanks, but we can't stay, really,'
and the telephone rang.

Arthur's forehead grew instantly damp with
panic, because the telephone was in the dining
room and anything over a furtive mutter would be
clearly audible here. And to go to the bedroom
extension, closing the door behind him, would look

peculiar. Very well; he would say, if the necessity arose, 'I'm sorry, you have the wrong number.'

He became aware that the telephone was still pealing, and that both the Saxons were regarding him curiously. He mumbled something and went rapidly into the dining room. The voice at the other end, when he picked up the receiver, was his brother-in-law's.

'If you've really made up your mind about this, Arthur, and you're going to be home, we might as well get the listing signed tonight. Somebody has to sell the house, and the sooner the better for you, I imagine.'

A very faint curiosity there, as to his speed in getting the house on the market? Surely not; no bereaved husband, especially one bereaved under the shocking circumstances, could be expected to cling to a house that held, in its wood and metal and fabric, the silent and ineradicable witnessing of violent death.

But if the call came while Richard Morley was here?

'Yes, fine,' said Arthur through dry lips. 'Any time that's convenient for you. I'll be home all evening. Give my best to Jennifer.'

In the kitchen, Ned Saxon solemnly accepted fifty-two cents, the two cents being tax, for his restoration of the bracket, and Iris Saxon said, 'I don't want you to think I'm going off with the silver, so will you please check this with me?'

She was light but firm, and 'this' being a large knitting bag, Arthur obediently but awkwardly looked in at a cloth tape measure, a cake of something to rub on irons, a pair of rubber gloves Mrs Saxon used when doing laundry by hand. 'And I think these are my scissors,' said Iris delicately—this meant she was certain—'but maybe you wouldn't mind making sure that yours are there, in that end drawer at the right.'

They were. 'Well, we won't take up any more of your time,' said Iris, sending a glance around the kitchen where she had put in so many days, 'but please'—her eyes began to brim—'please let us know if there's anything at all we can do.'

'That's right,' said Ned Saxon heartily, and the door chimes rang.

Instantly Arthur Pulliam had the liquor cabinet open. He seized a bottle at random, lifted down glasses that chattered perilously in his hands, said with a frantic hospitality that sat as oddly on him as a sarong, 'Oh, but you must have something. I really insist. Perhaps you'd just help yourselves while I see who—'

He had no plan as he hastened to the front door in a second impatient echo of chimes; he only knew that he must keep the Saxons captive in the kitchen for the next few possibly dangerous minutes. And after all that, and the panicky race of his heart, it was a weedy youth in glasses, a parcel delivery truck in the drive behind him, who said, 'Pulliam? Package for you,' and thrust out a flat rectangular box.

From the black and white zigzag pattern of the wrapping, and its next-to-nothing weight, the box contained some frivolity from Farrar's, a small costly specialty shop Molly had liked. Arthur put it down on a bookcase and, in his irritation at presently discovering that by some evil chance he had given the Saxons his most expensive Scotch, which they were sipping at as though it were vinegar, forgot about it until later that evening.

By that time Richard Morley had come and gone and the listing for the house, at an asking price of forty-five thousand dollars, was signed. 'I suppose you'll take an apartment for the time being,' said Richard.

Arthur shrugged. 'I haven't decided yet. Mr Heatherwood has suggested a leave of absence, and I think I'll take a week or so away before I do anything definite. That is, if the police . . .'

He almost unburdened himself to his brother-in-law then, even though there existed between them only the automatic civility of having married sisters. Richard Morley was tense, alert, sardonic-tongued, with a deplorable tendency to mock what Arthur considered the Solid Values; still, because of that very quality he might—

It was not caution that stopped Arthur's tongue, but a realisation that this was not the proper moment: Richard clearly had a problem of his own. His jaw, always aggressively taut, seemed now to be almost clenched, and in the last few days the sprinkle of grey in his close-cut fair hair appeared to have multiplied. As though he had read Arthur's mind he asked abruptly, 'Has Jennifer asked you whether Molly had been getting any peculiar telephone calls in the last couple of weeks?'

Arthur blinked in surprise. 'No, but you remember that the Sheriff went into all that—any enemies, or threats of any kind, and of course I said no. Molly would surely have told me at once.'

A flicker of cynicism passed through Richard's eyes. 'But did Jennifer ask you herself?'

'Certainly not,' said Arthur, beginning to feel obscurely offended. 'Why?'

'I heard Jennifer talking to someone on the

phone, and she seemed to feel . . . You remember
that picture of you and Molly the newspaper ran,
back in June sometime, with a small article about
your being feted, I believe the word is,' said
Richard, his raillery showing through even now,
'upon becoming a member of the Fifty Year Club at
Heatherwood Construction?'

'Twenty Year Club,' corrected Arthur stiffly.

'All right, Twenty. Jennifer seemed to have
gotten it into her head that either the picture of the
article might have had something to do with—what
happened.'

'I don't see that,' said Arthur in bewilderment.
He was so affected by the implied slur on the
Heatherwood Construction Company that he
whipped off his glasses and polished them angrily. 'I
don't see that at all. Besides, this fellow Baca . . .'

'Unfortunately, Baca's dead,' said Richard
Morley, and took his leave.

Surely, Arthur repeated to himself, Molly would
have told me if there had been anything like that—
but it was a train of thought his mind shied away
from and he took refuge in physical action, emptying ashtrays, checking the door locks, coming at
last to the black-and-white package.

Send it back unopened? But Jennifer had said
something about a coming birthday of her husband's, and suppose Molly had ordered—

When the tissue fell away the box disclosed a
blouse of very thin white silk, long-sleeved, starkly
simple except for an open and elongated diamond-
shape just under the high throat. Oddly for Molly,
an inveterate user of charge cards, it had been a
cash transaction, and the price was twenty-five
dollars plus tax.

The ordinarily frugal Arthur was not taken aback at that—he had liked his wife to reflect his own successful standing—but he was certain that a duplicate of the blouse already hung in Molly's closet, which again was odd because she had not been a woman to have two of such a thing. But this was female terrain; let Jennifer, who had promised to come and cope with the disposition of Molly's personal possessions, deal with the blouse as she wished. Arthur folded it back into the tissue, thrust the box into a desk drawer, and dismissed if from his mind.

He was—unknowingly, because he had never met her—much in the position of Eve Quinn when she had walked away from the problem of Ambrose's rockles.

Ambrose had temporarily forgotten about his rockles; he had a new absorption. So had Eve.

CHAPTER
FIVE

There was nothing in the envelope except the newspaper clipping, and even though there was no one but Ambrose to see her as she read it Eve could feel her face grow warm—not with hurt, or injured pride, but simply out of shock that someone who knew her should have seen fit to do this. While it was mischief on only a petty scale, it showed an attention trained closely on her.

The clipping was fairly long, headed by the photograph of a half-smiling girl with straight flowing blond hair, and it was datelined Chicago. It supplied the information that the engagement had been announced of Susan Hanes Griffith, daughter of, etc., and William Harper Cox, son of, etc. The schools and sororities of the bride-elect were gone into, along with her Junior League standing and her present activity with a children's charitable organisation; the history of William Harper Cox was similarly chronicled. An early wedding was planned. Well, naturally.

Almost oblivious to the fact that Ambrose had introduced a horned toad into the house, Eve looked again at the envelope, neatly and properly addressed, postmarked Albuquerque. Someone at the agency, obviously, because her own engagement had never been officially announced; it had been, she thought wryly, an inter-office affair in

every respect. It was the casual spite that bit, the
implicit hope that she would be reduced to tears.

In a world studded with real battle grounds, it
should not have been so shocking to discover such a
trifling enemy, but somehow it was. Someone—in
the typists' pool, in the production department, at
the switchboard?—had taken the time and trouble
to scissor the clipping, learn the new address Eve
had left in case any question should arise about
work she had just completed, stamp the envelope
and mail it.

Not Nina Earl, with whom she had shared the
travails of locally produced potato chips and
pickles; Nina was a friend and a good one. Certainly not Tom Sanders, who occupied the next
cubicle and toiled over an insurance company
account: 'The only company that enables you to
take it with you,' he declaimed occasionally. No; it
was a feminine gibe from someone contemptuous
at Eve for having let such a catch slip through her
fingers. The only person who came to mind was a
ravishing   copper-haired,   cream-complexioned
typist with eyelashes like stilettos over a green
glance which had been trained on Bill from the
moment he entered the office . . .

'At the door,' Ambrose was whispering hoarsely
and excitedly into Eve's ear. 'Oo, at the door.' Who
had encouraged him in these dramatics about
visitors?

Eve's first reaction, when she had opened the
door, was to whisk it closed again, because the man
who stood silhouetted against the grass and the
apricot tree was from Cox-Ivanhoe. She could not
fit the longish light-eyed face into any exact background, elevator or water cooler or one of the

green-carpeted offices, but she knew she was not mistaken. In her present frame of mind—she still held the spiteful little clipping in one hand—she did not feel cordial towards anyone connected with Cox-Ivanhoe.

She said unadornedly, in the tone she kept for aging youths purportedly working their way through college by selling magazine subscriptions, 'Yes?'.

His own look of polite recognition did not waver. 'I'm Henry Conlon, Miss Quinn. I apologise for the state you must have found this place in, but I've been out on the coast for a couple of months.'

Eve had been making out her rent checks to 'Estate of E. J. Dunn'; now, stunned and half-resentful, she realised that she was gazing at her landlord. Richard Morley might have told her—but of course, she realised even in her discomposure, there was no reason why he should; she had made no mention of the advertising agency, and certainly none of her broken engagement. With which, of course, this man would be familiar.

There was no recourse but to ask him in, and, once he was in, to ask him to sit down. Eve, made even stiffer by the Swiss-clock appearances of Ambrose's head around the doorway beyond her visitor's shoulder, said that she liked the house very much and that everything was fine. No, not at all; she had enjoyed putting the place in order. Yes, it was certainly a pleasant change from the city.

And with that a small silence fell. Eve was not vain enough to suppose that this mission was in any way connected with the agency; on the other hand, an apartment-dweller for most of her adult life, she found it unlikely that any landlord would drop around simply in the hope of hearing complaints about the pipes. She waited, and from the next room, clearly audible, Ambrose crooned silkily 'Come, my toad.'

Henry Conlon was polite enough not to look inquiring, but this interjection seemed to have the effect of waking him out of some inner preoccupation. He had been gazing about him in evident appreciation of the shell-like pallor of the walls, the cool gloss of the brick floor, the clean twinkle of the tall windows. It seemed to Eve that his glance had lingered unnecessarily on her typewriter on its table in the corner; it was an oldish Royal, and nothing to excite admiration.

Now he said, 'My aunt rented this house and lived in the one next door. The other executors want it put on the market as soon as possible, and as I'm the only relative on the spot I get the job of sorting a lot of personal stuff. So if you see lights over there now and then—'

'I did,' said Eve, thawing a little, 'and I did wonder. About vandals, I mean.'

In the next room, Ambrose abandoned his sugary approach and shouted angrily, 'Come, toad!' and this time it was too loud and too peculiar to ignore. Eve explained that she had a young cousin visiting her, and Henry Conlon said with a smile, 'With a friend, I take it. Do you by any chance have an older sister who went to school out here, the Lockwood School?'

The light eyes, Eve discovered, were a hazel-grey, and alert out of all proportion to such a question. She said no, no sisters at all, and Conlon rose. 'I have a favour to ask, if I may. I'm missing a key to the back door of the other house, and I wonder if it

got mixed up somehow with the keys here? In the
time of the last tenant I remember a brass bowl,
kept on top of the left-hand kitchen cupboard, I
think—'

Eve could not recall a brass bowl, but she said
obediently, 'Just a second, I'll look,' and as she left
the room the memory that she had been trying to
pin down flashed into place.

The last agency Christmas party. Cox-Ivanhoe
was not bothersomely big-happy-family, but the
copy staff were expected to make at least a token
appearance at this annual affair; indeed, many
people lived in hope of a repetition of the time
when heartily hated Mr Tannenbaum (Media) had
subsided into a huge bowl of fondue.

Eve, repairing her powder preparatory to leaving, had overheard part of a conversation between
two pretty secretaries.

'Oh, *him*. That's Mr Conlon. He's liaison, whatever that is. Tempting, I grant you, but you're just
putting a lot of mileage on your eyelashes for nothing. He's got a terrible down on women ever since
his wife.'

'Wife. Somebody up there hates me,' said the
other secretary moodily, leaning into the mirror to
examine her lipstick.

'Oh, she's dead, it was two or three years ago, but
that's the point. From what I heard—damn, why
doesn't somebody invent an elastic safety-pin?—
she was one of those females with a wandering foot.
Why she'd want to wander is beyond me, I'd have
been home putting new hems on his socks or whatever, but she did, and one night she took off with
some lunatic in his private plane, just for a lark, and
they were both killed . . .'

So that, thought Eve now, was what gave Henry Conlon his look of poised neutrality. It made an unassailable barrier, whereas bitterness was easily attacked.

There was no brass bowl on the cuboard top. Standing on the litle ladder, Eve was struck suddenly by the total silence of the house; it had a quality of held breaths, her own included. Well, Ambrose was probably waiting cunningly for his toad to betray itself. And Henry Conlon?

Very softly, from the direction of the living room, the silence was interrupted. There was a slippery rustle, a papery sound, the rustle again. Eve was deeply and instantly angry. Landlord he might be, but that did not give him the right to send her on fictitious searches—which now seemed obvious—and then invade her privacy. She walked swiftly into the living room, head militantly up. 'Mr Conlon—'

He was standing at a window, busy with a cigarette, every line of him expressive of polite waiting. *Could* the surreptitious sounds have come from Ambrose? She sent a rapid glance around the room, and felt an unreasonable heat rise to her face at the sight of the newspaper clipping which she had left inattentively on an end table. How she would appear to be brooding over her shattered love life . . .

'If there was a brass bowl, it's not here now,' she said levelly, 'and the only keys I have are the ones to this house. Sorry.'

His gaze flickered briefly—amusement at her warlike tone? 'Thank you anyway. I think your cousin has found his toad.'

'Oh? Well, it's not like the woman with the

drachma, I'm not going to call in a single soul to rejoice,' said Eve, giving him back his own detached smile. She moved purposefully towards the door.

'I gather you're busy,' murmured Henry Conlon.

'Yes, I am rather. Thank you for coming by.'

'May I say that you're very much missed at work?'

'That's very nice to hear,' said Eve, as glib as he, and closed the door behind him.

The first thing she did after that was crumple the clipping and toss it into the fireplace. The second thing was to find a shoebox for the horned toad, which Ambrose had indeed found swelling malevolently in a corner.

Eve had no love for horned toads, but even in her present preoccupation she felt a small and justifiable pride. Ambrose had come out here alarmed at houseflies; in her motherly zeal the usually sensible Celia had given him lectures on germs. He had screamed at his first encounter with a grasshopper, and stood paralysed when an elegant little lizard flashed over his bare toes in the garden. And here he was with a horned toad, harmless but certainly not attractive by any standards.

Eve, said firmly, 'You can't keep it, Ambrose, it will die,' but she helped him collect grass for the shoebox, and reclaimed the lid of a peanut-butter jar as a water dish. Ambrose enveloped himself in the straw hat and carried the shoebox out under the apricot tree, where he lay propped on one elbow and gazed fondly through the fringe at his hideous captive.

Eve returned to the living room and tried to

examine it through Henry Conlon's eyes. She had purposely kept the furnishings to a cool bare minimum—the little desk that held all her personal papers was in her bedroom—and the only object here of a remotely personal nature was her type-writer. And yes, his roaming glance had paused there.

As a shield against both the dust and Ambrose, Eve kept the typewriter covered; the cover, when she lifted it off, made exactly the slippery rustle she had heard from the kitchen. The sheet of paper in the machine was only the beginning of a letter to Celia, but in order to look at it Henry Conlon had concocted that nonsense about the key—had, Eve now began to suspect, come to the house at all.

And what was the random, out-of-context ques-tion he had asked her, dropping it in with that alert expression?

Ambrose, who steadfastly refused to take an afternoon nap and had once proved his case of wakefulness by reducing Eve's alarm clock to a jumble of tiny wheels and screws, occasionally betrayed himself by falling asleep. He had done it now, stretched out peacefully on the grass beside the shoebox. The hat had twisted wildly askew when he turned on his back, giving him somewhat the look of a diminutive drunk in a park.

Eve, obscurely troubled at being the object of unexplained curiosity, went to the telephone and called Nina Earl.

CHAPTER
SIX

'Now I wonder,' said Ned Saxon softly and for perhaps the tenth time, 'who Mr Arthur Pulliam didn't want us to meet?'

There was an edge of malice in the full and formal address, and Iris Saxon's eyebrows drew together. She had no particular liking for Arthur Pulliam, who struck her as pompous, but he was Molly's bereaved husband and as such, she felt, deserving of courtesy. There was no one to overhear them in the old car on this windy grey morning, en route to the Morley house for the first time since Molly's funeral, but she was uneasy at the lively speculation in which Ned had engaged ever since leaving Arthur Pulliam the afternoon before.

She said with unusual shortness, 'I can't see why you're making so much of a simple package delivery.'

'He was as jumpy as a witch before that.'

'It would be odd if he weren't upset,' reported Iris sharply. 'Can you imagine how the phone's been ringing in that house for the past few days?'

She regretted that immediately, because Arthur Pulliam's nervousness at the sound of the telephone had been almost a palpable thing, not the irritation or weariness that might have been expected. She snatched a quick side glance at her husband, but, intent on his driving or perhaps his own thoughts, he did not seem to have heard her. If Iris had been a woman given to flights of fancy, which she was not, she might have considered that he wore the gratified but deeply puzzled look of a magician who has pulled a live rabbit out of a perfectly normal hat.

Bothered by his expression, unable to put her own disquietude into words, she said crossly, 'It seems to me that for twenty-five dollars the garage might have taken a few more rattles out of this car. I keep expecting it to fall to pieces any minute, and how I'll get to work then I don't know.'

This time Ned did hear her, and glanced at her with astonished concern. 'Iris, what's wrong?'

The twenty-five dollars irretrievably spent two weeks ago, although Ned usually doctored the old engine himself. The cold fact, shocking to think about, yes, but still a fact, of having lost the small weekly income from the Pulliams. The knowledge that Ned would not allow her to seek any further such employment; the inevitable curtailment of the occasional drive-in movies that were their only recreation, the small weekend steak that constituted their one departure from a diet which could only be described as filling . . .

Habit was strong, and Iris managed a smile. 'Sorry—you know how this miserable wind gets me down. I'll be fine as soon as I'm busy.'

She was not looking at him then, she was automatically checking the contents of the capacious knitting-bag that went everywhere with her. Included in its depths was her own spartan lunch of an apple and some saltines spread with peanut butter; not even at Molly's had she ever accepted food, no matter how deviously offered.

The car halted in the Morleys' circular drive. Ned heaved himself out, rounded the hood, opened the passenger door and assisted Iris out as though she were the thinnest of glass bubbles. Together, like fond elderly children, they proceeded to the front door.

After a year of working weekly at the Morley house, Iris Saxon would have stood patiently in a blizzard rather than open a door that was not her own, even though Jennifer had said repeatedly, 'I wish you'd come right on in—some morning I might not hear you.' Equally, neither would Iris arrive at any but the front door: this was a fact understood by all parties.

Footsteps sounded within the house. Ned cleared his throat and said, 'I thought I might go from here to Center Cab. I understand they need drivers.'

He would go, and he would fall into a political argument with the manager or tell him kindly but firmly how he was mishandling the whole operation . . . Iris smiled with steady cheerfulness. 'Well, good luck, hon.'

Ned gave her a little salute of acknowledgment and an earnest blue glance. 'Now you be sure, if Jennifer goes out, to lock all the doors,' he said.

The footsteps were Richard Morley's, because twenty minutes earlier Jennifer had finished her breakfast coffee, looked at the clock, and stood up. 'If Iris comes while I'm getting dressed, would you let her in?'

Normally, on Mrs Saxon's day there, Jennifer indulged in a leisurely routine quite at variance with this businesslike air. A week ago Richard would have asked in surprise, 'Where are you off to so early?' Now he only glanced at her with cautious inquiry, unaware that his face had tightened.

'I'm going over to Arthur's,' Jennifer said abruptly, 'and get that over with. I should be finished by this afternoon.'

Molly's jewelry had already gone to the safe-deposit box, but there were still her clothes and the small intimate personal possessions, some of them dating back to her childhood, which could be neither discarded nor put into the hands of total strangers en masse. Appalled that they could be speaking to each other in these level and detached tones, Richard said, 'Should you be over there alone?'

'Oh, I'll be perfectly all right. It's something that has to be done, and the sooner the better. I'll see you tonight.'

It was crisp, arm's-length, dismissing as Jennifer herself disappeared and the shower began to run. And to Richard Morley there was something enormously wrong with it, even allowing for shock and grief and resentment at his delay in going to the Pulliam house on the night of Molly's death.

It was connected somehow with the mail.

On Saturday the mail had come late, around noon, and Richard had brought it in. Notes of condolence were still arriving for Jennifer, but there came a point in the envelope-opening when she turned so still that it was possible to think she had stopped breathing; it was the kind of stillness that had the effect of shattering sound.

Richard had said instinctively, forgetting his guard of the past few days, 'What's the matter?' and after a moment in which she stared at him as though he had addressed her in another tongue Jennifer had shaken her head. 'Answering all these people . . . it's going to take forever.' She had appeared to drop all her letters onto the table beside him then, as she always did, but nothing among them could have caused that instant of—dazedness? Disbelief? And late that evening, when she had thought him asleep, she had telephoned a man, although he had heard only the 'Mr' before her voice lowered to inaudibility.

The letter sender?

A less proud and fiercely jealous man might have questioned his wife point-blank even at the risk of a quarrel, or made some effort to find the communication which had stricken her into that silence. Richard Morley did neither. He saw the unprecedented gulf between them widen, was powerless because of his own nature to attempt to close it, and, on this windy morning, greeted Mrs Saxon briefly and departed for his office.

For all her appointment-keeping air, Jennifer did not leave the house at once. Noticeably thinner in a French-cuffed white silk blouse and charcoal skirt, even her lightest lipstick startling in a face grown angular, she made Iris Saxon a ritual cup of coffee and kept determinedly to brisk neutral topics. There was a small rip in the vent of Richard's dark blue suit coat, if Iris could get around to it, and might it be a good day to do the bedroom curtains? 'Hung out really wet in this wind they mightn't even need ironing . . .'

Although that was a waste of breath, because everything fell to Mrs Saxon's iron, including washcloths unless they were spirited away first. She was not a luxury, however, as Jennifer had often pointed out to Richard; if anything, she saved them money by laundering things which would otherwise have gone to the cleaner's—even raincoats emerged from her hands looking new—and effecting repairs which would have carried a tailor's bill. In addition, the finicky Richard's shirts now looked starched without being so, and retained all their buttons whole and intact.

'I'll be over at Arthur's if you need me for anything,' said Jennifer, 'and if anyone calls I ought to be back by three or so. Oh, and Iris, I'm sure they asked you this at the time, but Molly didn't have any unusual phone calls that day, did she?'

She was poking about in her purse with an air of abstractedness as she spoke, but she lifted her gaze quickly to the look of compassion in the older woman's face. 'Not that she mentioned,' said Iris, gently but definitely. 'She was—was just as usual.' Her voice threatened to tremble and she turned rapidly away. 'I'd better get busy, as you don't ask me over just for the pleasure of my company . . .'

So that compartment could be sealed off— couldn't it?

In the last few days Jennifer had taken refuge from thought by observing her own actions as though she were a critical stranger. Now, she watched herself get into her car and drive along the winding roads, spotted here and there with fallen yellow leaves, and slow presently for the turn into the Pulliam driveway. For a single undetached second she looked with revulsion at the old lilac, somehow smug with secrets even after its official investigation, and then she recaptured the protective mood, drove up to the door, used her key.

Get the easiest things over with first. True to his promise, Arthur had provided huge cardboard cartons, and in the bedroom, which seemed a special core of stillness in the silent house, Jennifer

folded Molly's suits and dresses and coats; by
arrangement, a charity thrift shop would collect
them. The more formal robes would go there too,
along with some layered-chiffon gift nightgowns,
still in their tissue—and like some horrifying klaxon
the telephone was ringing.

Arthur, of course; he had known she would be
coming today or tomorrow; still, it took a few
seconds for the unthinking fright to die away from
between her shoulder blades. And it wasn't Arthur,
but a woman who said to Jennifer's answer, 'Hello?
Is—hello?'

There was nothing wrong with the line. 'Hello,'
repeated Jennifer, and after a tiny pause the faintly
accented voice said, 'I'm sorry, I must have the
wrong number,' and there was a click and a hum.

. . . Lingerie, some cellophaned nylons.
Costume jewellery: Iris Saxon would probably like
some, out of sentiment, and Jennifer bundled it all
into the carved wooden jewel box now emptied of
Molly's good pearls and guard rings and the hide-
ously ornate ruby earrings which had belonged to
Arthur's mother. (And it was only eleven o'clock,
observed a treacherous portion of her mind; how
easy, once you put your mind to it, to pack and tidy
someone completely out of existence.)

Because there remained only the glove drawer,
and the half-used perfumes and colognes to be
thrown out, and—the thing Jennifer shrank from—
the contents of Molly's little desk, the letters and
photographs and other personal mementos which
for one reason or another she had kept.

'There might be some—ah—family thing you'd
want,' Arthur had said stiffly, 'or . . . I really don't
know, but I think it would be wise—'

He was right, of course; nevertheless, facing the task she had left until last, Jennifer found the chime of the doorbell a reprieve. She hadn't heard a car, although the driveway was gravelled like their own because of the dust. On the other hand, she hadn't been listening.

This would be one of those agencies which never heard of deaths in a family—a dairy soliciting its rivals' accounts, a newly established dry cleaner, an Indian from a nearby pueblo selling blankets or intricately worked turquoise and silver. Prepared to deal with any of them, Jennifer pushed her short dark hair back from her forehead and walked crisply through the depths of the house.

To her surprise, to her momentary fright, she opened the door on the totally unexpected figure of Ned Saxon.

CHAPTER
SEVEN

Her first thought, because of the atmosphere of disaster that lingered in this house like some terrible perfume, was, Something's happened to Richard. Then, mercifully, Ned Saxon gave her an anxious and apologetic smile.

'Say, I'm awfully sorry to bother you like this,' he said, 'but I saw your car outside and I wonder if I could use the phone? My car's conked out on me about a half mile down the road.'

'Of course, come in,' said Jennifer. She had none of Molly's embarrassment with the man; she quite simply and briskly did not care for him—personal hard luck was not always a guarantee of worth—but at the moment she felt a genuine compunction. In spite of the coolness of the morning the walk had been an obvious effort for him; his face, normally ruddy, had such a deep and almost radiant flush that for just a second, contributing to her momentary fear, he had appeared to be all one colour.

'I'd be glad to drive you to a garage if that would be any help,' she said, but Ned Saxon demurred at once with the air of deprecation which Jennifer always felt, without knowing why, to be completely false.

'Oh, I wouldn't think of it. I'm interrupting you as it is, I know. Fact is, I bought this old battery from a neighbour of mine and I think that's where the trouble is. He got me into this and he can get me out,' said Ned, smiling redly.

'Well, if you're sure . . . there's a phone in here,' Jennifer said, and turned and led the way into the dining room, because although Ned Saxon must of course know where the telephone was he would never make his way into the house without an escort. It was punctilious; it was also a nuisance.

His brief respite had quieted the breathing which had been laboured at the door. Behind her, his progress was utterly silent. So it wasn't an old wives' tale about bulky men moving with such delicacy, Jennifer thought absently, and jumped a little as the telephone burst into sound when she was two feet away from it.

It was Iris Saxon. 'Sorry to bother you, Jen, but there's a delivery man here with an electric broiler or something, and I didn't know whether you wanted me to sign for it or what.'

'Yes, would you? I forgot all about it. And by the way, your husband's right here, would you like to talk to him?'

Jennifer had turned automatically to face Ned Saxon when Iris's voice came along the wire; now, as she handed him the receiver, she was surprised and concerned about the ring of white around his mouth; he looked ill.

'Hi,' she heard him say as she walked back into the living room. 'You were right about the car this morning. I was on my way to that place on Fourth to see if I could pick up a lamp and it died on me . . . Right around the corner from here . . . That's what I was just going to do . . . I'll see you at five.'

The receiver went down, the dial spun, Ned Saxon delivered his complaint about the battery with the loud cheerfulness which accompanies rancor about a business transaction between friends. In the living room, he thanked Jennifer for the use of the phone. 'He's on his way, so I'll wait for him at the car.'

'I'll drive you,' said Jennifer at once. She might not—did not—like Ned Saxon, but it would have been impossible to turn out even a sworn enemy who was under such obvious stress. 'Just a second and I'll get my keys.'

But Ned would not hear of it. 'Iris'll have my head for barging in on you at a time like this,' he said, 'and besides, the walk will do me good. Maybe cut down the old avoirdupois, or do I mean embonpoint?'

He gave this its English pronunciation, drolly. Holding the door, then closing it after him, Jennifer doubted that the walk would do him good in any respect. Only extreme fury, which was ridiculous, or physical disability could have produced that startling red and ice-white countenance, and Ned Saxon was not a young man. Well, she had done her best. Like Eve Quinn, like Arthur Pulliam, she dismissed the matter and forced herself back to Molly's desk.

Nina Earl had been away on vacation, and Eve was not able to reach her until that evening. Ambrose was in the bathtub, still examining with sympathetic horror a wasp sting which he had received that noon and treated with perhaps two dozen band-aids, the peels from which Eve was still picking up in odd places.

Lively, talkative, immensely competent at her job, Nina said, 'Well, *you're* a voice from beyond.

Did you know we got the dog-food account, the one we sat up and begged for so prettily? *I* want some heartbreaking old piano music and a bloodhound or maybe just a basset eating sadly out of a bowl marked Brand X, with a Skye terrier or one of those happy eyebrowey types reveling in our stuff . . . Well, enough of this rubbish. What are you doing with all your leisure, besides not coming to see us?'

Eve considered explaining about Ambrose, decided that it was too complicated, and said, 'Nothing much . . . Nina, has Henry Conlon a sister?'

Nina Earl had been with the agency almost since its inception, and knew the life histories of most of its personnel. In addition, she had the kind of voluminous memory which could, if required, produce instantly the whereabouts and size of the nearest wildlife sanctuary.

She said now, with promptness, 'No. An older brother, I believe, an Army officer in Germany. Incidentally, he is a very nice guy, Henry, who has had a very rough deal.'

'He also seems to be my landlord.'

'Oh, is he? Well, you've probably heard that thing about a small world.'

'It sounds very faintly familiar. Was he ever connected with a school called Hapgood or Lockwood or something like that?'

'The Lockwood School for girls, and no, not that I know of. It went out of existence years ago, anyway, and small wonder.'

Eve, who knew that Henry Conlon's puzzling demeanour should by now have faded from her mind, felt her curiosity sharpen instead. She said,

'Oh? Why?' and then, as roars began to issue from the bathroom, 'Hold on a second.'

Ambrose, in the tub, had been trickling water lovingly over his head from a plastic squeeze bottle, unaware of the hazards involved. Soapy eyes shut, face scarlet with pain and wrath, he had already employed the bath towel, his pyjamas and his bath-robe, all of which were bobbing soddenly around in the tub. There was a considerable amount of water on the floor.

Eve brought him a dry towel and his only other pair of pyjamas, started and nearly fell on the wet tile when she received a venomous hiss from the newly escaped toad, and went shakenly back to the telephone.

Nina had heard the shrieks. She said coyly, 'Ah, you have news of an astonishing nature?' and Eve laughed. 'A cousin, with soap in his eyes. About the school—?'

But it was after all only negative information about an enterprise which had failed in spite of having contained, in the beginning, a lucrative idea. There was a good deal of money in the South-west, a lot of it new, and, in this immediate area at any rate, no really exclusive girls' school where along with the regular curriculum ranchers' daughters could be taught the vanishing arts of ballroom dancing and the pouring of tea and civilised conversation with their elders.

'But not a success,' said Nina, 'although it seemed to go along well enough for three or four years. Maybe there was too strong a flavour of silk purses. Anyway, it folded.'

'Quietly?'

'Certainly no headlines or I'd know,' said Nina

without false modesty. 'If it's important I could probably find out for you.'

Somehow all the urgency had drained away; perhaps that was Nina's matter-of-fact voice. 'Don't bother, it was just a thought,' said Eve, and they lapsed into the civilities of two women who had worked companionably together for two years. Nina said that the potato chip account had had to be talked out of an idea of their own—'Coulson's, the *hip* chip'—and that Mr Cox's pretty blond secretary had had twins. She went on chattily, 'Your local murder seems to have been solved, or shouldn't one bring that up?'

'Ideally, no,' said Eve; she had just become aware that the windows were completely dark and the curtains undrawn, and that for the first time in days she had forgotten to lock the back door. And under the rush of the bath water and the volume of Ambrose's shrieks . . . she said a hasty goodbye to Nina, agreeing to lunch soon, glanced in at Ambrose and proceeded to the door at the end of the narrow, galley-like kitchen.

The pane here looked directly across the wall and the shared driveway just outside it at the other house, and at some time since the fall of darkness Henry Conlon had arrived: there were lights on, capping the shrubs faintly with gold. Eve shook off the eerie feeling that her telephone inquiry to Nina Earl had summoned him up, turned the lock, and pushed at the bolt Ned Saxon had insisted on installing.

It was stiff, and as she struggled with it a car came wheeling into the driveway, its headlights vanishing before the motor was cut. Someone for her? It was hardly likely without a preliminary telephone call, but while Eve stood in doubt there was a dim flash of the courtesy light as the driver emerged.

Through the zigzag carving in the top of the gate let into the wall, Eve could tell only that the caller was a woman. She felt at once let down and embarrassed, because in a house which had belonged to his aunt and of which he was one of the executors Henry Conlon had a perfect right to entertain a whole procession of female visitors he chose—and then a woman, who had obviously forgotten something, returned rapidly to the car and opened the door for an instant.

This time she was recognisably Jennifer Morley.

Eve left the kitchen and returned to the bathroom where Ambrose, only his ankles in the tub and his face an alarming cherry red as he leaned out, was attempting to groom the cornered horned toad with her toothbrush. 'Stop that and get dry at once,' she said with unaccustomed fierceness, seizing Ambrose and the toothbrush.

'Brush,' said Ambrose just as angrily.

'Teeth, not toads. Oh, blast!' said Eve, and threw away the toothbrush, a new and very good one, and put Ambrose to bed with a grim speed that bewildered him into docility. 'My hat,' he only said meekly as she left the room, and Eve got the hat, placed it on his pillow, tiptoed out again with an elaborate silence suggesting that the little house was full of sleeping people, and had her own much-delayed dinner.

As the wife of the real estate broker who handled both these properties, Jennifer Morley naturally had matters to discuss with Henry Conlon, or rather commissions to carry out for her husband, and everybody knew that that business kept odd hours. As for the air of hurried anonymity, Eve had imagined that. Lots of people—people coming into very familiar driveways—switched off their head-lights even before they had finished braking.

In the road outside, a car had come to a pause with its engine throbbing. Eve ate her salad and devoted herself stoically to the book at her elbow. A little later, on the other side of the wall, Jennifer Morley's car backed, withdrew, and became a receding hum; it was followed at once by one which could only have been Henry Conlon's

None of it anything to do with Eve. She went briskly about her before-bed routine of straighten-ing the primitive kitchen and restoring the living room to its usual tranquility, but there was not the sense of accomplishment she had always enjoyed before in this small domain; something had been very slightly spoiled. It did not help when presently, she was unable to brush her teeth.

Not surprisingly to anyone even faintly familiar with him, Ambrose snored. Eve had overcome this obstacle to her own repose by imagining herself at a seaside resort, paying heavily for the privilege of hearing waves wash gently over pebbles. It did not work as well as usual tonight. Whatever the inter-pretation to be placed on Mrs Morley's solitary visit to the house next door, Eve wished that she had not been a witness. She wished too that Richard Morley, showing her the house months ago, had made even a passing reference to the executor's being a friend of theirs.

Not that it was her concern in any way, or so Eve thought until morning.

CHAPTER
EIGHT

It was not an auspicious day from the outset. Eve, who had had one of her rare broken nights, was tugged out of sleep by Ambrose's imperious hand to a whole assortment of unfamiliar sounds—rain—and the realisation that it was Iris's day to come and both the Saxons were at the front door, waiting in the downpour.

Ambrose could not reach the lock. Eve, not a fast efficient waker, said distractedly, 'Run and say I'll be right there,' and then in the strange twilight of the room could not find the sleeves of her robe. Barefoot, short fair hair pillow-rumpled, hating kind reliable Iris from the bottom of her heart, she fled to the front door and got it open, saying in an unstrung social way, 'I'm so sorry, I don't know what made me—Come on in it's *pouring*.'

The ever-courteous Saxons must have turned to each other the instant the lock clicked, because like two people in a comedy routine—apparently oblivious of the water streaming down Ned's face and siphoning off the folded newspaper held over Iris's head—they were offering each other measured observations about the weather. 'It's, what, August since we had a real rain? At least that. It'll be awfully good for the grazing.'

Into this strange scene Ambrose, half-hiding behind Eve, said in a very small but menacing voice, 'I want my rockles'. Simultaneously Iris shook out the newspaper and stepped inside, and Ned Saxon said in answer to Eve's invitation that he had to be on his way. Eve, very conscious that she looked decadent as well as disheveled in a robe and bare feet when the older woman had been up for hours, knew the depth of her own confusion when she almost imagined Ambrose saying in a soft and hair-raising voice, 'Is it dead yet?'

Like many mornings badly begun, it grew worse. Still somewhat bemused by the dark light and the million chucklings of the rain around the house, Eve started the percolator, showered, dressed, made her bed. When she emerged to announce that coffee was ready, Iris Saxon was seated in a corner of the couch, laying out her sewing kit and button box and rubber gloves as she always did, and Ambrose, planted in front of her, was saying coaxingly, 'Which hand?'

'Left,' said Iris absently, not looking up, and Ambrose popped the horned toad proudly into her lap.

Iris uttered a strangled sound of anger and horror, pressing herself violently back against the couch cushions. Eve, who had arrived just too late, cried, 'Ambrose!' and started forward. Ambrose bounded onto the couch with rocking force and recaptured his unwilling pet.

'Don't ever,' said Iris Saxon coldly out of an ashen face, when she had caught her breath, '*ever* do that to me again, do you hear?'

The woman and the child might have been alone in the room, and although a rebuke was certainly justified Eve felt queerly chilled. She had made up her mind the evening before that the toad had to go, if only for its own sake—but not in this shaming way. She said in a crisp light voice, 'Ambrose, you must keep him in your room or he'll get stepped on,' and, 'I'm sorry, Iris, he must have given you an awful fright. Come and have a soothing cup of coffee.'

'When they say boys will be boys,' said Iris, smiling wryly and recovering her poise, 'they know what they're talking about, don't they? It's silly of me to jump like that, but I hate those things . . .'

Toads, wondered Eve fleetingly, or little boys? A little girl, now, starched and ringleted and playing prettily with her dolls . . . that was unfair. She poured coffee into two cups, aware of Ambrose's silent and immensely baleful withdrawal, and was pleased when the telephone rang.

It was a wall arrangement, just inside the kitchen doorway. Eve lifted the receiver down, and a male voice speaking from what was audibly an office background said, 'Miss Quinn? Richard Morley. I hope I didn't catch you at a busy time?'

'No, not at all.'

'I hope the keys my wife brought you last night are the right ones,' said Richard Morley.

Eve's way here was certainly clear, after the first sensation of having been buffeted lightly in the midriff. No sensible person shored up such a deception between husband and wife; moral considerations apart, all it could reap was the blackest blame from both of them. It would take only a blank, 'What keys, Mr Morley?'

What she said was, 'I'm sure they are, although to be frank I haven't tried them—I'm just up.'

As traceably as air from a punctured tyre, the

tension escaped from Richard Morley's voice. Eve closed her eyes. 'Well, that's good,' said the voice in her ear, and then, perfunctorily, 'Everything else all right at the house?'

'Everything's fine, thanks.'

Feeling that her face must be a scalding colour, aware of a deep delayed indignation, Eve returned to the kitchen table and took up her coffee cup. She said to Iris Saxon with an air of bright recollection, 'By the way, have you any idea of what Ambrose means by his rockles? He keeps after me, and I haven't the slightest idea.'

(She was party, now, to a deliberate lie; the kind of person about whom she might have said surprisedly, 'Why did she do it? Why didn't she simply tell the truth then and there?' Why indeed?)

'Blocks?' suggested Iris alertly after a moment's thought. From her expression she might never have turned on Ambrose with the kind of contained savagery adults usually reserved for other adults. 'No, of course, he has those in his room. Rocks? But he doesn't collect them, does he?'

'No. It's probably something he's made up, or an excuse to get into the tool shed.'

(It would be nice to think, and it would place her in a more admirable light, that she had lied to Richard Morley purely out of compassion for his wife, who had just lost her sister under the most brutal circumstances. But it was only partly true.)

'It's a good thing that shed is locked,' said Iris, rising briskly with her cup and saucer. 'The trouble a little boy could get into there, with all those pruners and things . . .'

The wet morning deepened, and Eve blessed the clothes dryer which had seemed such an extravagance at the time. But the house was too small to hold Iris and Ambrose and the horned toad for hours at a stretch with any ease, and by eleven o'clock some break in the rainy day seemed imperative. Was it possible to play a restaurant against the toad?

Eve told Ambrose a long tale about the toad's wife and children appealing to her in the night; he liked things to be dramatic and no merely humane consideration would move him in the least.

'Crying,' he suggested helpfully when she had finished, his long eyes sparkling with sympathy or perhaps cynicism. 'All crying.'

'Yes,' said Eve, somewhat nettled, 'so I promised we'd send him home today. In fact, I said we'd bring him outside before we went to lunch.'

Ambrose was diverted at once; restaurant lunches had obviously been rare in his life. He insisted on being a partner in the release of his pet, and during a lull in the rain he and Eve decanted the shoebox in the chrysanthemum bed, leaving the box as an emergency shelter. In all this activity he had forgotten about the rockles, which was, thought Eve, a mercy. The tool shed looked more uninviting than ever with its sides streaked and glistening with rain; it was possible to imagine the spiders and other inhabitants working in a frenzy of dark and silent activity on this dripping morning.

The fact that Ambrose had dined in public very seldom was strongly indicative, and as she helped him get dressed, a process he was enormously particular about, Eve wondered where to go. The killing of time was an object, so was the lack of any large clientele. Someplace far enough removed

from the business district that it was out of bounds
for most people . . .

Courageously, at a little after twelve, Eve set out
with her problematical companion.

In his office at the Heatherwood Construction
Company, Arthur Pulliam was also having a difficult morning. On arriving he had told his
secretary, 'Absolutely no outside calls until I let you
know, Miss Haines.' He had then sent for several
files to buttress this statement, after which he had
sat staring at his leather-cornered blotter with his
neat head in his hands.

He was certainly safer at home, where he need
only lock the doors and refuse to answer his telephone; here he had only the doubtful protection of
Miss Haines, who like all timid people could be
hectored into submission by someone determined
enough, no matter what her orders.

He could take a leave of absence, as Mr
Heatherwood had suggested, but Mr Heatherwood
had suggested it with both distaste and disapproval—'Bite the bullet' was one of his gentler
philosophies—and in any case he could not go away
forever. A temporary vanishing from the scene
would be like turning his back on an animal of
uncertain, or rather certain, temper.

He had been unable to resist asking Jennifer last
night, very casually, if there had been any calls for
him at the house while she was there that day, and
she had said in her crisp noncommittal voice, 'Just
your broker, but I gather he was going to call you at
the office. And two wrong numbers, same voice. I
got the idea it was a professional pest.'

At this, Arthur Pulliam had nearly groaned

aloud. Now, he jerked electrically as his telephone rang. It was a summons to Mr Heatherwood's presence, and Arthur dried his palms and his forehead and swallowed a stomach pill in haste.

Richard Morley, meeting Mr Heatherwood once at the Pulliam house, had said disagreeably afterwards, 'They've been carving peach pits for years, I know, but it's amazing that they've got one to talk. What does he say at Christmas—ha, ha, ha?'

It was true Mr Heatherwood was small and intricately wizened, and held strong views about drinking, smoking, the eating of what he termed 'flesh meat,' Democrats, women who left their stoves except in a decent clerkly capacity, and many if not most ethnic groups. Nevertheless, he had advanced from nothing to a great deal of money, and Arthur Pulliam, who admired as well as feared him, resented his brother-in-law's gibes; it set his teeth on edge to hear the firm's president being referred to as Mr Leatherhead.

Usually Arthur attended these audiences pleasurably enough; although he was only one of three vice-presidents he was something of a favourite as Eugene Moles sometimes played golf on Sunday and James Sanderson had been foolish enough to admit to a deer hunt. ('Those dear innocent creatures,' Mr Heatherwood had said, closing his nutshell eyelids briefly before raising them again to write a sharp memo about coffee breaks. 'To be frank with you, my boy—who is this Mrs Pincus, who complains that her absenteeism is due to a hardship case?—I don't know how a man who calls himself a man could commit such an act.')

Mr Heatherwood often called Arthur 'my boy'. What would he call him if—?

But although he had confessed himself to be not pleased at the publicity for the firm in the matter of Molly's untidy death, Mr Heatherwood was affability itself; he even extended a ceramic bowl full of raisins. 'Well, Arthur. How would you feel'—he twiddled his swivel chair full circle to achieve maximum impact—'about stepping into second place? I mean it, my boy. The fact of the matter is that Jim Sanderson, for whom I have had the highest professional regard, is being divorced. And of course you know my feelings about that.'

The pill in Arthur Pulliam's stomach began to send out quivering tendrils. 'I'm sorry to hear that,' he began carefully. 'It's very unfortunate—'

'Unfortunate!' snapped Mr Heatherwood, and embarked on a ten-minute eulogy of a woman engaged in truly saintlike occupations, like serving on the Welfare Home board of governors and raising prize gladioli. 'And for such a person to be dragged through the humiliation of a divorce— well, we simply don't tolerate it at Heatherwood Construction, although we may be accused of being old-fashioned.'

There was an unmistakable crisping of his tone here, and Arthur found himself saying that he didn't think adherence to the moral laws should ever be criticised. He added that he hoped he would be worthy of the confidence Mr Heatherwood was placing in him and returned to his own office, which already seemed to have shrunk a little. He had green carpeting and chintz; Jim Sanderson had thicker carpeting, grey with matching draperies, plus a maroon settee and a flourishing rubber plant.

Miss Haines arrived in a flurry of interest. 'Oh,

Mr Pulliam, is it true about you replacing Mr Sanderson?'

'Changes in personnel always come from Mr Heatherwood's office,' Arthur told her distantly. 'If you'll bring your book I'll do some dictation now . . .'

Second vice-president, he thought as he worked. An increase in salary as well as in importance; a handsome bonus, certainly. Forget about Sanderson, whose private life had forced him out of this place in spite of his years of competence. With care, with planning, no one would ever—

Miss Haines had departed with her shorthand notes and was buzzing him on the interphone. 'I know you said no outside calls, Mr Pulliam, but the party claims it's an emergency. She wouldn't give her name.'

A hint of mockery there? Surely not; Miss Haines was much too meek, and besides—

'Very well, I'll take it,' said Arthur, pettish on principle although he now felt as though he had swallowed a very lively snake, and an instant later the dreaded voice was saying with sweetness, 'Arthur? Sweetie?'

CHAPTER
NINE

Like countless men before him, and countless men to come after, Arthur Pulliam could not fully have explained this disastrous entanglement even to himself.

Eight months ago, when it had begun, he had been a contented, successful, much-respected man, with an attractive home comfortably run by a wife who was pretty as well as fond and loyal. Into this unexceptionable situation, on the strength of her filling in for two weeks as his secretary when Miss Haines had pneumonia, he had introduced Rosalinda Lopez.

Molly was blond and plump and gay; Rosalinda was fierily dark and thin and had the temper of a cat with its tail being pulled. Pointed ivory face defiant, she had tossed badly typed letters on his desk at two minutes to five every afternoon; she might have been swinging back an invisible cape. Arthur, who had been worshipped by his mother and assorted female relatives, taken anxious good care of by his wife and tiptoed around by his secretary, was captivated. He said on the day before Christmas Eve, pretending to frown, 'Really, Miss Lopez—Rosalinda?—these letters can't go out this way. I'm afraid you'll have to do them over, and they must go out tonight. Oh, and if any question comes up, I'll be here for an hour or so myself. I have a few things on my desk to clear up, so you can come right in at any time.'

Rosalinda had been a beauty from the cradle, in her intriguingly scornful fashion, and understood perfectly. 'But I have a date, Mr Pulliam, and I'll have to call. What time shall I say?'

'Oh . . . better make it six-thirty,' said respectable Arthur Pulliam, 'because after working you so hard, and in the holiday season, I'll have to buy you a drink, won't I?'

As easily as that, it was begun. Rosalinda was as unnaïve as she looked, and knew that there was no question of divorce and eventual marriage; she did not even expect extravagant gifts. Born for display in handsome settings, she was content with an occasional excursion to Denver or Phoenix or El Paso.

Arthur was complacently shocked at himself. He was well aware without seeming to be that many people regarded him as reliable but dull, that Jennifer and Richard Morley thought of him as something that had more or less happened to Molly, like arthritis; that Molly herself would have crowed with affectionate laughter at the mere notion of his being unfaithful. He looked at his own sober album image when he shaved, and told himself that still waters certainly did run deep.

The affair had already begun to pall, and some coldly practical considerations to emerge into his hitherto dazzled consciousness, on that terrible night when Richard finally located him in Denver. Rosalinda was there at a nearby motel as a last—or perhaps next-to-last—gesture; Arthur had already made up his mind that he would end the thing. Rosalinda had after all known that nothing lasting could come of it and she was not a girl to spend her evenings knitting when she discovered him to be increasingly tied up by business—in fact, Arthur had a strong suspicion that that first date had been the result of a tempestuous quarrel with someone else. In any case she would speedily find herself another attachment.

In this frame of mind, he learned the appalling news of Molly's death. Even through the daze of shock and horror he realised that the impediment to possible marriage had been removed.

Marriage to Rosalinda Lopez.

The mere thought—let alone a vision of the Morleys, his friends, and his business colleagues; worst of all, his Wichita relatives—was so frightful as to make his glasses steam. In a sense, the impact of Molly's murder was cushioned; he would not be wholly given up to grief when he was already possessed by fear. Rosalinda had only to come forward and his life would explode. Not in a legal sense, as she was of age and he had been provably out of the state when his wife was killed, but she could still send him to a kind of grave.

Rosalinda did not come forward; with a delicacy he would not have expected she did not even send a note of condolence or any other communication. Arthur, at first weak with relief, began to realise that this was how volcanoes were born. Every ring of the telephone, every echo of the door chimes made him tremble because it would be Rosalinda with her implicit offer of marriage or ruinous headlines. Or it might even be her stepfather, a great hulking overalled brute whom Arthur had been careful not to meet but had seen at a distance.

Now, since his interview with Mr Heatherwood,

he had infinitely more to lose—and here was Rosalinda, saying in the purring tone which from her was
more ominous than a shriek, 'I've missed you so
much.'

'That's very kind,' said Arthur, patting at his
forehead with his already damp handkerchief.
'Actually, I'm rather tied up right now with
accumulated work. Suppose I call—'

'Oh, I wouldn't have to take you away from your
desk,' said Rosalinda, prettily deferential. 'I could
come there.'

So it had started. 'Wait, Miss Haines has just put
a memo on my desk,' said Arthur rapidly, 'and it
seems that—yes, I'm free for lunch after all. Could
you meet me—' He paused, riffling frantically
through his mind for a restaurant where they might
pass as tourists. Some place far enough away as to
be an unlikely spot for any of his fellow employees.

He did not now look in the least like a man
congratulating himself on the fact that still waters
ran deep, unless he were contemplating a pond with
Rosalinda at the bottom.

'—at Federico's?' he said.

Eve was pleased and surprised at Ambrose. True,
he had spooned ice back and forth from her water
glass to his with such tongue-protruding concentration that he had knocked over a small vase con-
taining a rose, but that was easily mopped up, and
although he had probed through his food as
thoroughly as though it had suddenly begun to tick,
he had done it quite neatly. Perhaps he was daunted
by the ill-lit and rococo splendours of Federico's.

It had been a wise choice. From the fact that the
women were hatted and gloved a good percentage

of the diners were tourists, deep in discussion about points of interest. As it was too expensive to be a family restaurant the only other child in evidence was a frilly little girl whose porcelain-statue behaviour threw Ambrose into a kind of brooding trance; Eve knew that there would be none of the terrible showing-off wars which could erupt without warning in public places.

Nevertheless, he had been amiable now for over an hour, and Eve was conscious of time running out. Although she had said it twice before, she repeated again, 'Don't let your ice cream melt, Ambrose.'

A man and woman had just entered the restaurant and were being ushered to a wall table. The woman had the faintly arrogant, arresting good looks of a model; Eve felt an odd little jump of recognition at the man. Although he might have been any insurance-company executive or Chamber of Commerce official he had looked at her from a newspaper page in another context quite recently. He was Arthur Pulliam, husband of the murdered woman.

A waiter presented menus. Federico's was dim indeed to someone who had just entered, and the woman, whose back was to Eve, put out a hand and switched on the wall lamp. Arthur Pulliam switched it instantly off. He leaned forward tensely and said something to his companion; she gave an easy shrug, consulted the menu, next consulted the mirror of her compact, and rose gracefully and strolled off towards the rear of the restaurant.

Arthur Pulliam remained seated, conveying an impression of deliberate rudeness rather than oversight. He gazed after the woman, and very fleetingly something transformed his neat inconspicuous face. Eve, who could not have helped watching, felt as though a cold fingertip had been placed between her shoulders.

Foresightedly, she had already taken care of the check. She said crisply to Ambrose, 'We have to go now. Napkin beside your plate, please—'

'I want this,' said Ambrose instantly, beginning to swivel his spoon wildly through his now-liquid ice cream. 'I want it!'

'Well, it's too late, I warned you before. And if you pick up that plate,' said Eve softly, observing his next move, 'I will spank you, in front of all these people. That little girl will see you.'

The last was a mistake. 'I hate her, I hate her!' shrieked Ambrose piercingly, and heads turned, forks paused, someone laughed. Eve, feeling herself to be the same terracotta colour as he was, smiled apologetically at an alarmed waiter and swept her charge off with his sneakered feet thrashing. Safely outside, she gave him a single resounding smack on the seat of his dark blue shorts. 'Don't do *that* again,' she said breathlessly.

Ambrose cried all the way home, but in a detached and practiced way; in the midst of his hiccups and the round tears speeding down his face he craned interestedly after a chihuahua, a helmeted boy and girl on a motorcycle, an immense old Indian woman in layers of gaudy satin. For her own part, Eve felt guiltily ashamed. Ambrose, not subject to a great deal of discipline at the best of times, had reacted to her reaction, and how was a boy of three to understand her instinctive recoil at the expression on a stranger's face? For that matter, how was she to understand it herself?

Except that his wife had been murdered a scant week ago, and his sister-in-law had paid a surreptitious visit to Eve's landlord, and Eve, through nobody's fault but her own, was now part of a distasteful lie. It was a little like the transmittal of a germ.

. . . When they left the house for lunch Iris Saxon had said, 'Have a nice time,' with an unmistakably commiserating wink, and out of loyalty to Ambrose, Eve stopped the car as they neared home and administered a handkerchief to his moist and streaky face. She was additionally glad of this precaution when she turned in at the driveway, because the Saxons' old car was there and Ambrose would have been exposed to two cool appraisals.

The rain had stopped but still held leaves and twigs and grass in tiny cool envelopes. Like an Easterner rejoicing in a flawless spring day, Eve stood inside the gate and enjoyed the chill, unfamiliar moisture on her skin; she did not even remonstrate when Ambrose plumped himself down on the lawn and rendered himself barefoot.

Ned Saxon was proceeding to the tool shed as she rounded the corner of the house, and she was inspired to call, 'Could you wait while Ambrose goes in with you for a minute, Mr Saxon? He thinks he left something in there.' To Ambrose's upturned and wide-eyed face she added, 'Hurry up—now's your chance.'

The kitchen was full of a warm cinnamon smell and Iris Saxon's face was oven-flushed; as usual after snapping at Ambrose she had made him some confection. The high colour accentuated her clear eyes and gave her a disarmingly girlish look. 'Have a nice time?' she asked, rinsing a mixing bowl.

'Very. Ambrose was as good as gold,' said Eve. It was, after all, ninety per cent true. (As though, she thought wryly, anything less than the truth were anathema.) 'Whatever that is smells wonderful.'

'Well, I didn't think you'd mind if I rummaged around for this and that. They're only cinnamon buns with raisins but I thought the little boy might like them for dessert tonight. And before I forget, Jennifer phoned. Jennifer Morley,' Iris said as Eve looked blankly back at her.

'Did she leave a message?'

'No, she said she'd call later.' If Iris was at all curious it didn't show. 'And a man—wait, I wrote it down . . .'

It was no surprise at all when she produced the pad on which she kept punctilious notes of calls and the man was Henry Conlon. Eve felt a wave of illogical anger at having her own folly thus made concrete and handed to her. 'Will he call back too?' she inquired edgedly.

Iris looked mildly surprised at her tone. 'He didn't say. The mail came, I put it in on that little table in the living room.'

Both the Saxons had a rooted conviction that mail left in a box for more than sixty seconds would be stolen by villains in search of social security or other checks. Eve thanked her and went distractedly into the living room. A rose-scented advertisement which she dropped into the waste-basket unopened, her telephone bill, a thick letter from a friend in Baltimore with whom she maintained a curiously undying, once-a-year correspondence, and a postcard for Ambrose from Celia—printed, ridiculously, as though Ambrose, who could not read at all, would have a little less trouble with printing.

Motherhood, the great leveler, thought Eve with irritation. On the other side of a view of a duck pond in Central Park Celia had written fatuously, 'Hi, darling, we miss you! Mama is getting better every day and Daddy sends his love,' And who wrote this thing anyway, wondered Eve blackly—one of the ducks? 'Tell Aunt Eve I will call around eight p.m. on the nineteenth. Hugs and kisses.' Well, really. On the whole, in Eve's present mood, the telephone bill made more civilised reading.

It was a long afternoon. Iris Saxon explained in her scrupulous way that Ned had come at all because the bathroom window, difficult in any weather, had swollen in the rain and refused to close, so Ned had planed it. 'Water was coming in all over the floor and I didn't know what to do.'

The rattling old car departed, to return at five. Ambrose came in beaming and muddily barefoot to exhibit an old spark plug. 'Saxon gave me,' he said proudly, turning it on his palm with admiration.

It now seemed safe to ask, so Eve did, 'The rockles weren't there?'

Ambrose gave her a brief look of fright before his face cleared. 'All gone,' he told her reassuringly, and nodded his silky head for emphasis. 'All gone.'

Eve was pleasantly surprised at Ned Saxon's masterful use of psychology. Somehow he had convinced Ambrose that he was well rid of the unknown treasure—which of course could not have been there in the first place—and supplanted it with a new one. She was also relieved that there would be no further exhortations to enter the shed. Spidery places were unattractive at best, and her determined avoidance of this one for the past few days had turned it from a shabby little outbuilding to the repository of some kind of triumphant evil. It was almost as though the tool shed knew it had gotten the better of her, and might make use of this knowledge if she were so unwary as to undo the padlock and step inside . . .

The Saxons' car arrived punctually at five o'clock. Eve had to listen for it, as Ned Saxon would never do anything so peremptory as sound his horn and Iris would certainly not start glancing at the clock as the afternoon drew on; if anything, she commenced on entirely fresh tasks at that point.

Eve said now, 'Your car's here,' and Iris replied serenely, 'just let me finish this button,' and did. Moments later Eve slipped the folded check into her hand—a check seemed somehow less like a naked exchange of money—and said as always, 'Thanks, Iris. Now we'll be presentable again for a week.'

'And we can eat, which is even nicer,' said Iris, laughing, and put on her coat and departed with a wave into the unfamiliarly early twilight. Eve, waving back and closing the door, felt a pang: would she herself, no longer young, take extreme adversity so well?

Ambrose was flushed with the excitements of the day, and could be depended upon to create some noisy scene if he were not fed and put to bed early. He presaged this by announcing belligerently that he would not take a bath and Eve couldn't make him. 'All right, no bath,' said Eve equably, and set about preparing his dinner. A portion of her attention waited for the telephone to ring, but apparently whatever Jennifer Morley or Henry Conlon had wanted to say to her was not very imperative.

Good, said Eve to herself, crumbling well-drained bacon into macaroni and cheese sauce for Ambrose's favourite meal. Nobody wanted a land-lord on the premises, and Mrs Morley could only be calling in connection with the incident of last night. Firmly, Eve wanted no further part of that.

She had brought Ambrose his fruit gelatin and more milk when it was borne in on her that she was taking a ridiculously high moral tone; sitting in judgment, in fact. She had liked Jennifer Morley on sight, and, if she were to be humiliatingly honest with herself, she would not have felt that barely curbed anger all day if Henry Conlon were old or fat or even a supple and dazzling Romeo.

It was not a pleasant revelation about herself, and to mitigate it at least she would return Mrs Morley's call. Eve was delayed by the shattering crash of Ambrose's dessert plate; while she was picking up the pieces the silent telephone came to life.

But it was neither of her previous callers. 'Sorry to bother you,' said Ned Saxon's voice against a background of bustle and pinging cash registers, 'but Iris didn't leave her glasses there by any chance, did she?'

'Just a minute, I'll look . . .' The couch where Iris sat when she sewed, the tabletops, the kitchen counters—'They don't seem to be here, but I'll keep an eye out,' said Eve, returning to the phone, and hung up.

Ambrose, still barefoot, could not be allowed to climb off his chair and into the needle-like splinters

into which the plate had burst: even the thought of
his outcry at such an injury was insupportable. The
slippery dessert, with its banana slices, would
hardly make an adornment for the rest of the house
either. Eve cleaned it up laboriously and said to
Ambrose with only passing terseness, 'Yes, you
may turn on television. Please do.'

So that it might have been six o'clock or even a
little later when she dialed the Morley's number,
half-hoping that it would be unanswering or busy.
But Jennifer Morley's voice said immediately,
'Hello?'

'Eve Quinn, Mrs Morley. Iris Saxon told me you
called today while I was out.'

'Yes, I did. A guardian of my morals saw fit to
call my husband about seeing my car in your driveway last night. I did use your name, and I apologise
for that, but I wanted to explain that you weren't
conniving at something wrong. The fact is that
Henry Conlon and I—'

At that point Jennifer Morley's attention was
abruptly withdrawn. Her voice came back an
instant later, saying rapidly, 'Someone at the door,
but I'll get rid of whoever it is. Could you possibly
hold on, because I do want to talk to you?'

'I'll hold on,' said Eve, and the receiver was
placed delicately down on wood. Airiness after
that, the special hollow quality of a listening
mechanism, so that she heard the sound of a door, a
distant, 'Really? Are you sure . . . ?' from
Jennifer, and then airiness again.

Eve lit a cigarette and waited, more out of politeness than curiosity; as far as she was concerned the
conversation had already accomplished its purpose. The car that had paused in the road while Mrs

Morley was inside the house next door had obviously contained 'the guardian of her morals'—but why assume her whereabouts so accurately, when it was in fact a shared driveway?

In any case her own indignation at being used had abated under the forthright tone of the other woman's voice. She finished her cigarette, however, in mild annoyance at people who laid receivers down and forgot about them, although she had done it herself more than once under the pressure of a last-minute, scrap-everything burst of work at the office. She was about to hang up—only preoccupation had kept her from doing it earlier—when she heard the other phone come alive against wood.

As Mrs Morley did not say, 'Sorry to have kept you,' or anything else, Eve said crisply 'Hello? You're obviously busy right now, Mrs Mor—'

Gently, with no emphasis, the receiver clicked into place. Eve listened in amazement to the dial tone before she hung up: this was something that rarely happened between rational adults. And then she realised what must have happened: Jennifer had not been able to get rid of her caller; her husband had arrived and, finding the phone off the hook, replaced it without even lifting it to his ear.

It wasn't important. Eve was relieved merely at having made the gesture, even if she had made it for the sake of her own conscience. Any further move would have to come from Mrs Morley, and somehow, the awkwardness dissolved even without explanation, she did not believe there would be one.

In this she was quite right. Jennifer Morley would never speak to anyone, about anything, again.

CHAPTER
TEN

Even Iris Saxon would have been astonished at the speed with which her bulky husband could move. Replacing the telephone receiver with his gloved hands, holding the record of Eve Quinn's voice even through the intoxicating pound in his ears, Ned Saxon slipped rapidly through the front door, stepped into his shoes, crossed the gravel, was into his old car and away.

Another one, he said about dead Jennifer to his blood. Another one of the easy-living women whose deepest worry in life was weight-watching, and who handed his wife—his wife!—their broken slip-straps to mend, their laundry to wash, their idly expensive clothes to iron. 'Oh, thank you, Iris. I don't know what we'd do without you, Iris. And by the way, if you get a chance, Iris . . .'

And for all their handsome homes and their fine manners they were so stupid. They looked upon him as an adjunct of their nicely brought-up servant, and never saw him as a man at all. Molly Pulliam, for example, had assumed that he had come to fix the bracket under her kitchen shelf; why else would lowly Ned Saxon presume to knock even at her back door?

And yet it was Molly Pulliam who had shown him the pattern that had undoubtedly been there all along, the pattern laid down in his very blood. He would have seen it for himself quite soon, but the matter of the blouse had hastened things.

Two weeks ago—or three? Time had assumed a curious elasticity lately, and Ned could not be sure—Iris's eyelids had been pink and swollen when he picked her up at the Pulliam house. 'One of my allergies,' she had said lightly to his anxious question, but later that evening when she thought him fully absorbed in the newspaper she had drawn something from the depths of her knitting bag and gone to work over it at the towel-padded kitchen table that served as an ironing board. It was a white blouse of some delicate fabric, with an odd-shaped cutout in front and the beginnings of a wedge-shaped scorch which all Iris's frantic spongings were not remedying in the least.

In the account which she could no longer avoid, the picture became so clear that Ned clenched his hands as he listened: Molly lying down with one of her rare bad headaches, Iris answering the telephone so that it would not disturb her and returning to the ironing board to find too late that the iron had somehow overheated; Molly wailing when Iris showed her the blouse, as she did instantly, 'Oh, Iris, I wanted especially to wear that tonight with my black dinner skirt.'

My black dinner skirt—for some reason that alone brought the bile to Ned Saxon's throat so that he had to turn away.

He chose not to believe in the headache—why should comfortable waited-upon Mrs Pulliam have a headache?—and to ignore his wife's 'It made me feel even worse, the way she kept trying to make up for it all afternoon. She's always so sweet, and you couldn't blame her really because it is a lovely blouse. I thought maybe scalded milk—'

But nothing availed against the scorch. Iris sadly

threw the blouse away; Ned retrieved it secretly, took twenty-five dollars from their tiny savings and went to the shop where it had been bought.

Farrar's was all thick pale grey carpeting, with scarves and costume jewellery tossed carelessly over pieces of driftwood, and saleswomen who looked like young dowagers. In Ned Saxon's mood of grim rage it was almost pleasurable, and by the time he had persuaded a particularly haughty woman to take his money, all of it, and write out an order, the pattern of what he had to do was beginning to emerge. It was helped along by the preliminary, 'Will this be cash, sir?' Farrar's obviously would not trust a check from him although they would have bowed and scraped over Molly Pulliam's.

Iris's swollen eyes, and distress at the mere recounting. If she had tried to keep this from him, what other private humiliations had she suffered at the hands of people protected from all harm by a checkbook? And how they probably talked about her, *Iris*, and said, 'I have this marvellous woman who comes once a week, she can do everything. She's not the kind of person you'd expect to find doing this kind of work, but her husband's out of a job and they're really up against it.'

Kind and patronising, from a safe distance, and Iris really *liking* these people, in her innocence, and not suspecting their mockery at all. She was like a child exposed to vicious adults, and Ned Saxon was exposed too.

He could not have said at what point wish became intent. He was dazzled by the springing up of the pattern, which seemed his alone, something new and bold and as urgent as vaccine against a crippling disease.

He said nothing to Iris about the purchase of the blouse—unnecessary, he saw that now—but explained the expenditure of the twenty-five dollars as a garage bill. (Some day he could tell Iris what he had done on her behalf, but not yet. She was a woman, after all, and emotional.) He continued driving her to the homes where she was degraded and demeaned, and he listened more attentively to her naïve reports, such as, 'Molly's going to a cocktail party at the Fletchers'.' He had a kind of hugging delight, worth more than any money in the world, in abasing himself before these three women, because he thought, Soon . . . soon.

He had almost had Molly Pulliam on that first occasion when he had waited in the lilac, just as he had almost had Jennifer Morley yesterday when she turned her back on him in the empty Pulliam house and Iris had chosen that exact moment to call. For a blind second then he could have destroyed Iris herself, who was primarily Mrs Ned Saxon—

But tonight had been simplicity itself. Iris had genuinely misplaced her glasses, something she often did, and the timing of the call to Eve Quinn had struck Ned as obscurely useful in some way. Leaving Iris with her barely begun shopping and search for 'specials' he had said, 'I'll get the eggs, shall I?' because since one malodorous egg they never bought them at the Maxi-Mart. 'If you would,' said Iris, peering nearsightedly at applesauce, and Ned was off.

He had bought the eggs on his way to collect Iris—they were on the floor of the back seat concealed by a sweater—and he took the ditch road, something not many people would have attempted in that particular car, so that he arrived at the

Morley house a good ten minutes earlier than if he had taken the conventional route.

There was no house opposite; only a tacked-up For Sale sign on land for which, in this area, an exorbitant price was asked. Nor was there any immediate worry about Richard Morley arriving, even if it had not been his firm's weekly sales meeting night; he was often late and there was no finger pointed to intimate knowledge there.

And if on the off-chance that he came in just this small space of time, Ned Saxon was simply passing by in humble pursuit of his wife's glasses; Eve Quinn could bear that out.

To Jennifer Morley, who opened the door with an air of impatient haste, he said with his usual air of geniality, 'Say, I happened to be driving past and I wondered if you have a workman here or something?'

'No, why?'

'Well, someone just dodged around the corner of your house, and it seemed to me—' It did not matter what he said, as she would never repeat it.

'Really? Are you sure . . . ?' Dauntless because she had a man with her, as arrogantly militant as all her kind, Jennifer Morley rounded the house with him, peered into dripping darkness, said, 'Do you think you could take a look for me? I'm on the phone—'

It was too late by then to abandon this opportunity, because she had turned and looked at his face. With his hands, because of that intrusive child in the tool shed, Ned Saxon killed her.

She was enormously strong, much stronger than her sister; at one point in that very brief struggle she struck at him with a piece of stiff wire she had seized up in the second of realisation. The near miss made his hands jump reflexively on her throat, so that she was able to gasp out of a darkening face queerly lit by the light from the kitchen, '*You killed*—'

She could not seem to get her sister's name from her contorted mouth.

'Yes,' said Ned Saxon, and finished his work and, before she could fall, supported and half-carried her to the little belt of trees which Richard Morley was always promising to thin out. There was a long half-rotted beam there, and the remains of an outdoor fireplace. Ned Saxon dropped the unresisting body behind the crumbling stone structure— Jennifer Morley would not have thought his breathing quiet now; he was taking great panting lungfuls of air—and sped back to the telephone. Thanks to the perilous ditch road he was back in the supermarket twenty-five minutes after he had left it, saying to Iris, 'I got the eggs. Extra-large, they were all out of the jumbo.'

Richard Morley did not attend the weekly sales meeting because it was his turn to sit in an open house from six until nine. Even if the evening had not been rainy this was an almost certain waste of time—the house was overpriced and suffered badly from what the real estate manuals called, rather grandly, functional obsolescence—but it belonged to a friend of the firm's president and living sacrifices had been made to it all week.

As the property was in the Heights there was no point in going home first. Richard Morley called Jennifer at five-thirty and departed for his lonely vigil. The rain was coming down in earnest now; nobody in his right mind would be shopping for houses, not even the usual assortment of time-killers who liked to peer into other people's domiciles when there was nothing of interest on television.

The house was furnished solely by a straight kitchen chair and an old paperback which Richard pounced on hungrily and dropped with disgust when he found that the last chapter had fallen out. He might have been the last survivor of some great disaster: on one side the darkened identical mate to this place was also for sale; on the other side was a weedy corner lot ornamented with beer cans and fragments of glass. Presumably the other residents of this deteriorating street drove forth occasionally, but they were not doing so tonight.

Normally this whole situation would have reduced Richard to savage gloom, but now he sat down quite mildly on the kitchen chair, glanced at his watch, and gave himself up to pleasant thoughts about the irony of Mrs Mincer.

Mrs Mincer and Jennifer were old foes, dating from a time when Mrs Mincer's brass band of guinea hens had invaded the Morley property and been attacked with zest and appetite by Jennifer's German pointer puppy. Mrs Mincer, an elderly and razor-tongued widow, had not unnaturally called up in a trembling rage; Jennifer had retorted with some justice that those strident and witless birds were a public nuisance. So *she* might think, said Mrs Mincer triumphantly, but according to the law fowl-killing dogs were required to be confined. 'Very well, then, and I'll get a restraining order for your horrible guinea hens,' Jennifer had answered furiously, but she knew when she was beaten. Rather than chain the puppy, or have him shot or poisoned by Mrs Mincer, who was thoroughly capable of it, she had sorrowfully found him another home.

Since then the two women had been implacable enemies, and it was Mrs Mincer's acid voice which had called Richard at his office to say, 'In your own interest, I think you should know that your wife has been visiting that man at the Judd house, that bachelor or widower or whatever he calls himself. At least, her car was there last night.' Click.

In the scene which was thus precipitated—Richard had gone home to lunch, because he did not want Jennifer unarmed against Mrs Mincer's venom, and his own difficult nature tore at him—they had arrived at almost their old accord. Jennifer had said she had brought duplicate keys to Eve Quinn—'She said something to Iris the other day about wanting them, and she's an awfully nice girl, don't you think?' and added casually, 'It'll disappoint Mrs Mincer but it turns out that I do know Henry Conlon, from years ago in Colorado. I had no idea that he was still in this part of the country until—he read the newspapers, of course, and he sent a note . . .'

The note that had driven her into that white stillness, and which he had never been shown? For the moment Richard did not ask; he was too relieved that for the first time in a week Jennifer was looking at him as someone other than a stranger to whom she must force herself to be polite. And with that new beginning, anything else could be straightened out. Anything . . .

Arthur Pulliam had, very unusually for him, gone to a movie.

He was so preoccupied with the terrible problem

of Rosalinda that he saw only strange disoriented images on the screen: a man in a raincoat, the spinning wheels of a train, a woman in what appeared to be black lipstick dropping a sinister capsule into the drink of her companion, who had obligingly turned his back.

Rosalinda had been far from good-humoured at lunch, but what worried Arthur even more was the frequency with which she had dropped her black lashes. She—or that stepfather of hers—had worked out some ferocious demand, and she was simply testing him, like a woman poking a fork inquisitively into a roasting chicken. She was obviously not ready to spring her ultimatum, because when Arthur had begun stiffly, 'I'm sure you can see that this is hardly the time—' she had interrupted him in her most catlike tone. 'Of course I can see. I'm not stupid.'

'Then why . . . ?'

There was a brief interruption as a child began to shriek and was carried out bodily. 'I missed you,' said Rosalinda then, reverting to blandness and giving Arthur a ravishing look from her eye corners. 'Naturally.'

Six months ago, even three months ago this coquetry would have enchanted him. Now it seemed to turn the lunch he had scarcely begun into a jumble of broken glass nestled intimately in his stomach. If only he dared announce firmly that any further meeting between them was out of the question—but he did not, and when they parted it was with the understanding that he would call Rosalinda soon.

At any rate Arthur was safe for the moment in this flickering anonymous dark; he could not be telephoned or confronted by anyone. Even the massed and rapt attention around him—the woman on the screen was now dragging her comatose victim to an open elevator shaft—was somehow comforting, simply because no one was staring at or speculating about *him*; nobody was whispering, 'It wouldn't be the first time a man hired someone to get rid of his wife . . .'

Eve Quinn listened to the rain with active pleasure. Ambrose was asleep, the kitchen was tidied, the little house, thanks to Ned Saxon's planing of the bathroom window, impregnable to this enjoyable wild night. She had had her shower and barely begun an engrossing book. It was one of those rare intervals of perfect tranquility and anticipation, not to be thrown away by going early and mundanely to bed. She was even thinking that in some strange way she would miss Ambrose when the knock came at the door.

It wasn't late, just nine-thirty, and Eve was cautious but not frightened. Her robe was an almost monkishly austere white wool, not a frilly just-out-of-bed creation, and when she went to the door, secure on its bolt and chain, she asked crisply through the crack, 'Who is it?'

'Henry Conlon . . . I apologise for coming so late,' he said, entering, 'but I was on my way home and it occurred to me that I ought to—that you should have some kind of explanation.'

Eve flushed; she felt as though she were standing in her kitchen again, looking out, spotlit. She was saved from having to answer by the ringing of the telephone.

It was Richard Morley. After the first terse question Eve wheeled unthinkingly to gaze at Henry Conlon, and in some way it was as though his pleasant spiky-eyelashed face were enormously familiar instead of seen here only twice. She said into the telephone, 'No, she isn't . . . Yes, she did, but she didn't leave a—Yes, I did, around six, but your wife had to answer the door, and when she came back she hung up. I suppose she was in a hurry and took it for granted that *I'd* hung up . . .'

She replaced the receiver, and said shakenly to Henry Conlon, who after her first wordless turning to him had made no pretense of not listening, 'that was Richard Morley, and his wife seems to be missing. Her car is there, but apparently she had no dinner and there's no note or anything . . . he's calling the Sheriff now.'

Missing: it was odd how a single word could seem to sweep aside adobe and glass and fabric and introduce the rainy black night almost physically into the room. Conlon's face had gone frowningly tight and—Eve was to cling to this—disbelieving. Whatever he had been going to say before the telephone rang had obviously been wiped from his mind. 'I'll go over and see if I can help,' he said.

Help meant search, of course. Eve felt cold even before he opened the door. 'I'll be up for a while. Will you let me know if you find out anything?'

In spite of the dripping obscurity, and the tendency of tree branches to throw suggestively shaped shadows just outside the patiently moving lights, it was not a very long wait.

CHAPTER
ELEVEN

'She must have walked out of the house voluntarily,' said Henry Conlon, wearily and for perhaps the fifth time, 'or you'd have heard.'

Eve gazed at him through a woolliness of shock and pure physical and nervous fatigue. Although she had not glanced at the clock lately she knew it must be after midnight. They sat in her living room, talking in low voices so as not to wake Ambrose and absorbing the new fact of Jennifer Morley's death by strangulation very possibly, almost certainly, when she had been in the middle of talking to Eve on the telephone. The crisp voice saying, in a ghastly turn of speech, 'I'll get rid of whoever it is.'

As Eve would not have left Ambrose alone in the house at even an innocuous and sunny hour of the day, a deputy had come to take her statement that she had held an interrupted conversation with Mrs Morley at somewhere between six and six-thirty, that the dead woman's last audible words had been 'Really? Are you sure?' and that there had been no further sound of any kind before the receiver was replaced.

Jennifer had obviously expected to be outside only momentarily as her body, when they found it behind the stone fireplace, was clad only in blouse and skirt. Still clenched in her right hand was a piece of stiff wire which, for all its exposure to rain, was sent off to the laboratory; it was possible that she had marked her killer.

The deputy wanted to know if Mrs Morley had sounded in any way frightened or alarmed by her visitor, or if on the other hand she had seemed to be addressing a friend, and Eve discovered for the first time how difficult it was to assess such a thing when you were armed by hindsight. The very importance of her answer, and the resulting tendency to strain for nuances, was a heavy stress to place on four unremarkable words.

'She sounded impatient, if anything,' Eve said with care, 'but then it's always a nuisance to have someone knock at the door when you're on the phone. Of course, I wasn't really paying that much attention at the time.'

'No, you wouldn't be. Did you have some special reason for calling Mrs Morley, Miss Quinn?'

'No, I was returning her call—I'd been out earlier in the day but as I was home from two on I don't think it could have been anything very pressing,' said Eve steadily.

Henry Conlon, who had been silent and alert on the other end of the couch, saw the deputy out and returned to the living room doorway. 'I don't like to sound openhanded with your liquor, but I think we could both use a drink,' and was soon making efficient sounds in the kitchen.

The question of why in Jennifer Morley's death was almost as baffling as the question of who. You thought of the husband right away—but according to Conlon, Richard Morley had seemed stricken almost to the point of physical collapse. Nothing in the house had been touched. Someone had come to kill, done it, and gone away satisfied.

Eve had never met Molly Pulliam, but on the basis of an admittedly slight acquaintance Jennifer had seemed an unlikely target for murder. Probably only newborn babies had no enemies to any degree at all—Eve thought of the casual malice directed at her in the form of the newspaper clipping that announced Bill Cox's engagement—still, enemies who *killed*?

As though it had accomplished its night's work, the wind had died; there was only a reminiscent plop of rain here and there, mockingly peaceful. Ambrose gave an occasional dim snore. Conlon gave Eve a peculiarly measuring look, came to some inner conclusion, and said, 'You've known Nina Earl for quite a while, haven't you?'

'If two years is quite a while, yes.' As the import of this question was borne in on her, Eve felt a trace of wry amusement at the thought of their both, and separately, having used Nina as a character witness. It was, in its way, quite a tribute to her.

'I knew Jennifer very well, years ago in Colorado,' Conlon said abruptly. 'Her sister Molly was younger, and for some reason I hardly knew her at all—I certainly never connected her with a Mrs Pulliam. I'd been living in New York for years before I came back out here, and I'd lost touch with the family completely. Then Jennifer called me up a few nights ago to find out if I was the same Henry Conlon. She'd just had a very unpleasant anonymous letter, touching on something that happened a long time ago, and she wanted to rule out the possibility that the writer could have had anything to do with what happened to her sister.'

'*Wanted* to rule out . . . ?' repeated Eve incredulously.

'Yes, because it didn't seem possible for a lot of reasons, and to go to the police with the letter would only have stirred up a lot of unnecessary mud. She wanted me to make some inquiries because she had never told her husband about this matter and it would have been—awkward. Jennifer didn't say as much, but I gather that Morley is a very'—he seemed to search before he went on—'single-minded man, by which I don't mean jealous in the ordinary sense. Although, all things considered,' said Henry Conlon, meeting Eve's eyes levelly and speaking with a certain dry calm, 'I think I am probably one of the safest men living as far as anyone's wife is concerned.'

Because of course, his own wife . . . Much to Eve's relief, Ambrose could be heard in an excited and rising mumble. Nothing of this night's frightful happening could have penetrated to him, but she went swiftly into his little room, turned him on his side, said softly, 'There's your hat.'

Ambrose was not really awake, because when she nudged the straw folds gently into his hand he responded, 'There's my hat,' and succumbed again. Thoroughly roused, he would have wanted a drink of water or a trip to the bathroom or something to eat. Nevertheless, Eve waited for his gentle tidelike snoring to recommence before she returned to the living room and Henry Conlon, who asked, 'Did I wake him?'

'No, he often does that.' In her brief interval away Eve had had time to think, and she said with conscious politeness, 'I gather, then, that Mrs Morley thought I might be the anonymous letter-writer, because I was about the right age or would be if I had an older sister? That was why you wanted to look at my typewriter?'

'Jennifer was hardly at her most clearheaded,'

said Conlon in mild reproof. 'All these years had gone by without a worry about—what she was worried about. Then you turn up in this particular house, which is listed with her husband's firm; you even have the same woman in to help.'

'Yes, I see. Well, there's no great mystery about that,' said Eve with the terrible pleasantness that only underlines anger. 'Mrs Morley herself suggested Mrs Saxon to me, and as for the house, I was completely unfamiliar with the Valley so I consulted our good and mutual friend Nina—who would, I suppose, have known about this place?'

(Nina Earl with her vast lack of surprise that Henry Conlon had turned out to be Eve's landlord, her carefully off-hand endorsement of him. She would take care of Nina later.)

Henry Conlon, who had clearly arrived at the same conclusion, took out his embarrassment in a long astonished glance at his watch before he got to his feet. The living room froze briefly around Eve like a stopped film, but she managed to say, 'I hope you convinced Mrs Morley that I didn't write to her, and that I've never been near the Lockwood School.'

The room froze deeper. Henry Conlon said out of a great and crystal silence, 'Yes, I did. Thank you for the drink. Goodnight.'

Where fatigue had been, there was now a furious restlessness. Nonsense, thought Eve, and began turning out lights. She looked in at Ambrose again, half-hoping he would raise one of his unseasonable commotions, but Ambrose would not help her; his lashes were peacefully down, his wide mouth, that was capable of such disarming and sharklike smiles, open to facilitate snoring.

Eve used her new toothbrush, took two aspirins and went to bed. It was the kind of night she liked best for sleeping: cold enough for blankets, musical with the aftermath of the rain. Burned against her eyelids almost until an ambitious rooster came to life was the photographically clear image of Henry Conlon's left wrist, extended as he looked at his watch, and the end of a fresh scratch there.

The morning newspaper said in a black banner 'Sister of Valley Victim Slain.' There was a lead paragraph in heavy type, and the usual head-and-shoulders presentation, in a vital and confident pose, of someone freshly dead. In stores and offices and trailer courts there was a deep hum of shock and anger, even though Jennifer Morley had not been as widely known or uncritically liked as Molly Pulliam—and under the hum ran a clear little current of relief.

The murder of Molly Pulliam had been a matter of personal terror for and posed a threat to them all—what other door would this madman force, what other lone woman select for his prey?—but this was something else again. The violence was not random after all, but directed at the two sisters by some sort of reason, or something which a warped mind had construed as reason.

Nevertheless, it was entirely possible that the killer came and went among friends of the dead women—smiling, handing or accepting drinks—and delicately, self-protectively, the people who had been so shocked and angered began to disavow this dangerous pair. The very women who had gathered over their midmorning coffee to vie with each other as to their closeness to Molly now said consideredly, 'Of course, I didn't know either of them really *well* . . .'

'Jennifer was always rather a lone wolf, wasn't she? I mean, she kept herself to herself pretty much . . .'

'I've barely met Arthur Pulliam—he's not terribly friendly, do you think?—but I was at a party a few weeks ago when someone said something to Richard Morley that he disagreed with, and you won't believe this but he walked right out of the room, leaving poor Maude Fellowes with a whole handful of drinks. Naturally I couldn't feel sorrier for him, they were a really devoted couple if I ever saw one, but it does show temper, doesn't it? Not that he could possibly . . . I'm not suggesting for a minute . . .'

This dainty knifing was only a reflection of the official attitude. At the time of Molly Pulliam's murder, the Sheriff's office had automatically verified her husband's presence in a Denver motel. They had also put a few perfunctory questions to Richard Morley—perfunctory because, even apart from an apparent lack of motive his air of horror in that sauerkraut-smelling house, and frantic concern for his wife's reaction, had seemed unarguably genuine.

Moreover, the Valley was not the city with its element of unknowns who had drifted in yesterday and might drift out tomorrow. Here, most of the residents were taggable either by sight or by reputation, and both the Pulliams and the Morleys were alien to such a brutal crime on both heads. If there had been rumours of dalliance anywhere, or a financial straitening with insurance involved . . . but neither circumstance obtained.

And Silverio Baca had turned up, with his wrathful mutters about his former employers, his record of theft, his drinking bout. He had fitted in as neatly as the missing piece of a jigsaw puzzle, but someone had turned the puzzle upside down. Grimly the Sheriff's officers began to restudy Arthur Pulliam and Richard Morley, and the past of the women who had begun life as Jennifer and Molly Vane.

CHAPTER
TWELVE

There was one coincidental factor that the Sheriff wanted tidied out of the way, one common denominator to note down as having been examined and dismissed. Accordingly, early the next morning, a deputy made his way to the tiny apartment where the Saxons lived.

Although a scant ten-minute drive would have taken him to either the Pulliam or the Morley house, this was a sharply different world. A year ago, even cloaked in deep tree shadows, the street had shown the marks of poverty; now, with the blighted Chinese elms cut to stumps, the sunlight stared cruelly down on small cement-block structures stained with reddish dust around the bases, exposed gas meters, defeated lawns gone back to hard weed-sprouting earth. Children had played with and abandoned a few old inner tubes, and against one crumbling pale green wall was a black dog so thin that he might have been a mural.

The deputy knew Mrs Saxon slightly. He was also familiar, in a different and tolerant way, with Ned Saxon, who had called in indignantly on various occasions to report a Peeping Tom, a sheared-off mailbox, strange small-hours trafficking across the street. There did seem to be a bewildering number of people at the address in question, and the mailbox had undeniably been wrecked, along with several others on the block, but under the circumstances the deputy could not place much faith in the Peeping Tom.

It was Saxon who opened the door now, with an expression that startled the deputy until he caught sight of Mrs Saxon; she was obviously in a very shaken state and her husband did not want her further upset.

'Come in,' said Saxon, standing aside. He was holding the newspaper, and he shook his head at it. 'I don't suppose there's any new lead in this terrible business?'

'Not yet.' Invited, the deputy lowered his large frame into a chair which gave an alarming twang. He kept his gaze firmly riveted on Mrs Saxon in order not to look about him, because he often found himself in surroundings of extreme financial depression but they seldom embarrassed him to such an extent. Perhaps it was because these people were so proud, and so far from young.

He said gently to Mrs Saxon, who was gazing at him like a child who has been savagely punished for no reason within its comprehension, 'We're trying to find out all we can about Mrs Morley's activities yesterday, Ma'am. I understand that you were at Miss Quinn's when she telephoned there—would you remember what time that was?'

The tiny frozen turn of Ned Saxon's orange head was arrested so swiftly that it went unnoticed.

'About one o'clock,' said Iris Saxon a little unsteadily. 'I told her that Miss Quinn had taken the little boy out to lunch, and we chatted for a few minutes and she said something about having errands to do and that she'd call back later. But she didn't, while I was there.'

'And you got home at about—?' This was the real

point the deputy had come to establish, even though it was an almost purely academic one: all other considerations aside, it seemed laughable to the point of tragedy that these hard-pressed people would have wiped out any source of income.

'It must have been well after six,' said Ned Saxon, with a consulting glance at his wife, who nodded, 'because we did our week's shopping and if you've ever been in the Maxi-Mart on double-stamp day you know what it's like. Tell you what, though—the manager would probably know what time we left there because when we were at the checkout stand it seemed to me that a package of noodles looked funny, powdery, and he gave me kind of a hard time about it and kept looking at his watch. You've got to be very careful about the freshness of packaged foods in those big markets because sometimes,' he explained severely, 'the boys who restock the shelves don't do it properly.'

This was evidently a hobbyhorse of Saxon's, along with Peeping Toms and hypothetical drug traffic, and the deputy—who was now listening to something about an earlier purchase of eggs at the Double A Egg Ranch—began to be afflicted by a monumental boredom. Hastily, before he could be lectured about the hazards inherent in buying eggs, he left. A routine check would have to be made, but this angle, never of much interest to the Sheriff's office, had been taken care of . . .

The deputy's car cruised away, its departure attended by gaping children and a few inquisitive women. Ned Saxon closed the door and said softly and fixedly to Iris, 'You never told me that Jennifer had called yesterday.'

'Why should I?' asked Iris, her eyes beginning to

fill. 'It wasn't important, and with—with what happened it went completely out of my head.'

Like his departure from the Maxi-Mart, supposedly for eggs—but he had not been able to chance leaving that out of his account to the deputy. He had actually bought the eggs forty-five minutes earlier than the time stated, but it had been darker than usual because of the rain, and in any case the clock in the sales office of the Double A Egg Ranch stood permanently at twenty minutes after eight.

'There,' said Ned tenderly to his now weeping wife. 'There, Iris. They'll catch the man, because it stands to reason that women like that—'

Iris's bent head lifted unbelievingly, almost angrily.

'—young, attractive, might have made enemies without knowing it,' continued Ned in a smooth flow. 'The newspaper said they came originally from Colorado. You wait and see, it'll be somebody from there.'

'But that won't bring them back,' Iris said in a drowned voice.

'No,' agreed Ned, gazing tranquilly over her shoulder. 'Nothing can do that.'

'There was a letter,' repeated Richard Morley exhaustedly, 'which upset my wife very much. It came on Saturday, and that's all I can tell you about it.'

To this particular deputy, who ruled his family with an iron hand, it was almost inconceivable that a wife should withhold mail from her husband, even more so that the husband should not have demanded the letter on the instant. He said skeptically, 'And you think that this letter may have had a bearing on your wife's murder.'

'I think it came as a direct result of her sister's murder, and the two have to be tied up, don't they?'

Richard had not slept for well over twenty-four hours, and all his taut aggressiveness had drained away. He was docile under this questioning, even though the deputy had the kind of personality which would normally have touched off his low flash-point, and he seemed completely unaware that he was being viewed as a possible double murderer even when he was examined once again as to his activities the evening before.

'So nobody showed up at this empty house you were sitting in. Somebody must have seen your car there—it was visible from the street?'

'Yes, but if you've checked up on the place you'll know that there's another empty house on one side and a vacant lot on the other, and the store that sells wigs across the street. It was closed. Besides which,' said Richard with a first faint anger, 'it was raining cats and dogs, if you'll recall, and I imagine that no one was out who didn't have to be.'

'You seem to have bad luck with your business in the evenings. Let's see, on the night Mrs Pulliam was killed some people broke an appointment to look at a house with you, didn't they?'

Verification of that other appointment, at this late date, had proved impossible; the people concerned were from a small town in the southern part of the state, and even if they could have been contacted in their apparently leisurely tour it would have proved nothing. Morley could have seized the unexpected opportunity to go to the Pulliam house where he knew his sister-in-law to be alone.

But even this did not seem to penetrate. 'Officer,' said Richard Morley wearily, and began a dissertation, singularly contained, for him, on the state of this particular business in Albuquerque. The few men who were not real estate brokers had wives who were, he said, and women in this field had as many scruples as piranhas when it came to pirating other people's customers. As for the other aspect, there was the tale, which no one could be sure was apocryphal, of the would-be buyer who had thoughtlessly spent his down payment in a cigarette machine.

In the middle of this indictment Morley's attention had begun to stray; he was trying to make up his mind about something. The deputy had seen the signs before—the tightly locked fingers, the focused stare that saw nothing but some abstract weighing of a possible good against a possible evil. He waited prudently, and Morley said slowly, 'I don't think it will help, but the only thing out of the ordinary in the past few days—apart from the letter—was that my wife had discovered that an old friend of hers was living here in Albuquerque. Not far away, in fact.'

This was more like it, thought the deputy, concealing a flash of elation; this was the first crack in the happy unimpeachability of these two households—because there could be no doubt, from the other man's tone, as to the sex of the old friend.

'His name is Henry Conlon,' said Morley, 'and you can reach him . . .'

Unlike his brother-in-law, Arthur Pulliam was openly shocked and shaken when asked to account for his whereabouts at the presumed time of Jennifer Morley's death. He said in a horrified voice, 'You can't possibly think that *I* had anything to do with this terrible business? Good God, she was my wife's sister!' Another thought struck him then. 'I can't believe that Richard means to insinuate, just because Jennifer spent a good part of the day before yesterday here, helping me with the disposition of my wife's personal belongings, that there's any reason whatever to—'

He floundered here, and not because he had lost the thread of his sentence. It was clear that this was the first investigating officers had heard of Jennifer's lengthy and solitary presence in the Pulliam house, and that they were extremely interested.

They had done the routine photographing and finger-printing at the time, but because of the apparent nature of the crime and the fact that that short and terrible chase had stopped well short of the bedroom, they had paid little attention to that area beyond having Arthur Pulliam verify that his wife's jewellery and his own valuables were intact. Certainly it had occurred to no one to dredge through the closets and bureau drawers and the pretty little desk which Arthur now indicated to the deputy.

But Jennifer Morley had done just that, and been strangled two days later. The two facts might be totally unconnected; on the other hand, they might have the tightest possible link.

Attention went back, temporarily, to Arthur Pulliam and his movie, and it was at this point that the deputy's curiosity began to stir. It was not so much that the other man could not remember the name of the movie and was not even sure of the theatre—'It's somewhere on Central'—as his obvious perturbation. He took off his sparkling glasses and polished them as vigorously as if they had just emerged from the bottom of a mud puddle, and although explanation of his own motives was clearly something that did not come easily to him, he embarked on a long string of propitiatory phrases.

His own recent loss . . . tried to bury himself in his work and had perhaps been overdoing it . . . sometimes a movie, even a bad one, was the best way to relax . . .

Which might be true, except that it hadn't worked very well for Arthur Pulliam, thought the deputy. Had he had a female companion with him, to whom he didn't care to admit? That would be interesting even if not criminal, and some of these solid, board-meeting types were the very ones . . . but he looked again at the neat respectable face and thought, No.

Some overriding worry on his mind, then, which had driven him to a movie he could scarcely remember this soon afterwards? Or simply grief and strain, as he said? Certainly Pulliam was unbreakably alibied for his own wife's murder, unless—

In any sizable city there were areas in which desperate men could be bought for any purpose. It seemed farfetched, as there was no apparent reason why Pulliam should have wanted his wife dead, but unless and until something turned up in Colorado the two husbands were the only line to pursue.

As in the case of Molly Pulliam, there was next to no physical evidence to go on. Gravel did not take tyre prints, even if the killer had come by car; again, if it had been he who replaced the receiver after Jennifer Morley had laid it down to go out to her death, Richard Morley had used the telephone, and the whole area of the desk on which it stood, to call friends in search of his missing wife before notifying the authorities. An understandable procedure, but not helpful.

Neither man bore any fresh cuts or scratches, but in view of the preliminary lab report it now appeared that Jennifer Morley had missed her assailant. Still, the interviews had not been barren. Richard Morley was disturbed about his wife's 'old friend,' and Arthur Pulliam had been flustered.

Easy enough to look into Conlon; the deputy made a dubious note in his report as to the advisability of, maybe, having a closer look at Pulliam's extracurricular activities. Through the services of an uncle of his by marriage, who had worked at the Heatherwood Construction Company for years, this was to have mildly surprising results.

CHAPTER
THIRTEEN

Eve woke that morning with the sense of disaster that had followed her into sleep and coloured her fragmentary dreams. She was not yet conscious enough to remember the cause, and when she first opened her eyes she thought it was something to do with the bewildering change that had come over her bedroom in the night.

Where there should have been shafting sun, there was a strange greenish twilight, and the window across from the bed was an unfamiliar mass of leafy darkness. Eve had been so deeply and exhaustedly asleep that she had to prop herself up, blinking, before she realised that at some point a huge cottonwood branch had come down and was pressed against the panes. And if she had not heard that—

Was that smoke on the air?

Fortunately, even without smoke, there was seldom any doubt as to Ambrose's whereabouts; when he was busy at some totally silent activity it was in a hivelike way, constituting a cone of its own in contrast to the innocent silence of chairs and tables. At the moment he was absorbedly burning slices of bread in Eve's horizontal toaster—this was still a novelty to him—and there was a neat black pile beside him.

'You shouldn't do that,' said Eve, limp and inadequate in her relief. 'It's a terrible waste of bread for one thing,' she added a little more briskly.

'For the birds,' suggested Ambrose sweetly.

'Birds don't like burned bread.' To Eve, fully awake for not quite a whole minute, it seemed incredible that Ambrose could have been so active so early, but he had. The refrigerator door hung open a few listless inches, a carton of milk was leaking on the floor, there was a knife buried up to the very tip of its handle in the peanut-butter jar.

First things first: Eve disconnected the toaster over Ambrose's angry protest, put coffee water on, went back to her bedroom for the robe she hadn't bothered with in her precipitous dash. The bowered effect lent by the leaning branch had a kind of eerie charm, but she supposed she would have to—

Memory came back then, of the reason for the late evening, her exhausted sleep, her sense of catastrophe upon waking. Somewhere in this glittery morning Jennifer Morley's body was being dealt with; equally, a murderer with strong hands was still sleeping, or having breakfast, or going briskly off to work. Unless—

Eve brought her clock-radio into the kitchen and listened to it with a screening ear while she opened the windows and tried to wave out the layered blue smoke from the toaster, mopped up the spilled milk, rescued the peanut-buttery knife. She surprised Ambrose, on her entrance, backing out of the broom closet in a flushed and disconcerted way and clutching a crumple of sheeting to his chest.

It had come, Eve realised, from the box where she kept rags for cleaning; she had to conceal them from Iris Saxon, who out of her own desperate need

for thrift would have sewed or patched them indefatigably together. A memory flickered through
her head and was gone. Ambrose held out the cloth
and said in a tone of simple command, 'Wash it.'

Eve broke two eggs into a bowl and beat them
with a fork. 'It's already clean, Ambrose. It's a torn
pillow-slip that got into the laundry yesterday.'

'*I* wash it,' said Ambrose, and he sounded so
fiercely anxious that although she could already
look ahead to the resultant mess Eve said, 'All
right, but hurry up, I'm starting your scrambled
eggs.'

The only news about the murder of Jennifer
Morley, when it came on, was negative. The
Undersheriff said that every available deputy had
been assigned to the case and 'we will work over-
time on this thing.' Asked if it could be definitely
assumed, in this light, that the appearance of
robbery in the earlier crime had been a diversionary
tactic, he said with official caution, 'It's one of the
lines we're working along, yes.' With scarcely a
pause a caroling commercial began, and Eve
clicked it into silence.

She had lied by omission, the night before, in
giving the impression that the interruption at Mrs
Morley's end of the line had come almost immediately. She had made no mention of that wry 'Some
guardian of my morals' or 'The fact is that Henry
Conlon and I—'

How would that have continued?'

'—are old friends' would have been Conlon's
version. Eve hadn't seen the scratch on his wrist
when she gave her statement, and she avoided to
herself now the question as to whether it would
have made any difference. Inevitably, since the

matter of Bill Cox, she had a strong disbelief in feminine intuition; still, she found it impossible to believe that Henry Conlon would kill anyone, let alone a woman.

Richard Morley, now, with his barely controlled tension—

Aghast at herself, Eve called Ambrose for his eggs and toast and cocoa, and went outside to hang his pillow-slip remnant on the line. Now that she thought about it, which she was only doing to escape her other thoughts, he had had another favourite piece of cloth not long ago, with a small oblong of vivid print, looking not unlike a pocket, patched onto it by Iris Saxon. Ambrose hadn't sucked on it, or taken it to bed with him, or put it to any of the other legendary uses of small children with such objects, but he had been extremely fond and careful of it. Eve had not seen it lately; undoubtedly Iris had washed and ironed it and folded it into the depths of the linen closet.

. . . As to scratches, Henry Conlon's might have come from anything at all—a cat, a protruding nail, a bent piece of chrome on his car. Eve herself, somehow immune to injuries as an apartment dweller, was constantly discovering on her own person, now that she was taking care of a house and child, bruises and small cuts and burns which she had no recollection of incurring, simply because she had been too busy and involved at the time.

It was not the happiest train of thought.

By only a little after ten o'clock, the sun was so strong that except for a glimmer of silver on the underside of a leaf or in the tremble of a spider web, it might never have rained. Roads and driveways would be puddled, and the lawn damp, but

Ambrose was certainly able for that. In spite of the cold nights there were still grasshoppers leaping springily about, and Eve cut holes in the lid of a coffee jar and suggested that Ambrose capture some to put over the wall.

'Why?' asked Ambrose, sensible and staring.

'Because they like it over there and they can't fly high enough. We have to help them.'

'Can't fly, we *help* them,' said Ambrose, captivated, and set off on his task.

A throaty voice at Nina Earl's telephone advised Eve that Mrs Earl was at a meeting; could she take a message? Yes, if she would, said Eve, attaching a face to the voice instantly; would she have Mrs Earl call this number? 'Oh, and I want to say thanks for sending the clipping about Mr Cox's engagement. I mightn't have seen it otherwise.'

There was a thunderstruck silence—the receiver, certainly, pressed under the beautiful coppery hair. 'Tell Mrs Earl there's no terrible rush,' concluded Eve gently, and hung up. That was one small mystery resolved.

Ambrose, looking like a straw hat which had grown legs, toiled away after the grasshoppers which sprang elusively in every direction. Eve did the breakfast dishes, grateful to have her hands and at least the very surface of her mind occupied; she even cleaned the overworked toaster. The muffled sound of a car door closing did not seem to have any relation to her until someone rapped briskly at the front door.

It was the deputy of last night. Ambrose lurked at his heels, fearful but fascinated.

'I wonder,' he said after shaking his head at Eve's

first instinctive query, 'if you might know where I could find Mr Henry Conlon? I've checked his home and his office, and I thought maybe you had—'

He broke off politely as the telephone rang. Eve, going to answer it, had time to realise that this question was not really surprising: Conlon's presence here late last night had created a natural but false impression. In her ear, Nina Earl said briskly, 'Eve? For heaven's sake, what's going on out there in the woods?' Unaware that Eve was in any way involved, she barely paused. 'After you brought up the Lockwood School the other day I happened—'

'Oh, pretty well, thanks,' Eve broke in brightly. 'How's Dave?'

Dave was Nina's husband. There was a short astonished pause, into which she said somewhat testily, 'Apart from having been carried off by a gorilla, fine. I take it this means you can't talk right now. Call me back, why don't you?'

'I certainly will,' said Eve, still social and airy. 'Thanks again.'

Logic had known that she could have received information and even have asked cautiously framed questions about a subject which had produced that sharp reaction in Henry Conlon, and the deputy would have been none the wiser. Instinct had been afraid.

Returning to the living room, she said, 'Sorry . . . No, I have no idea where you can reach Mr Conlon if he isn't at his office.' To the unspoken comment that they had appeared to be on fairly close terms the evening before, she said, 'He's my landlord, you know, and he happened to be here when Mr Morley telephoned last night.'

'I see. Well, he'll turn up,' said the deputy agreeably, and Ambrose, usually shy with strangers, reached up and tugged imperatively at the leather holster just within his reach. 'I have a bug,' he announced, holding up the coffee jar.

'So I see.' The deputy tweaked the hat from Ambrose's head by its conical crown, inspected Ambrose, and clapped the fringed straw back on. 'That's a fine-looking hat,' he observed soberly, and thanked Eve. 'I don't suppose you've remembered anything further about . . . ?' He broke off, disconcerted by the unwinking regard from below.

Eve said no, but she would certainly let them know at once if she did. She thought as she closed the door that she could give a very good guess as to where Henry Conlon was.

Ambrose had tired of chasing grasshoppers and, before the patrol car's motor had died away, demanded to go to the store. 'Maybe this afternoon,' Eve told him distractedly. She remembered to add on her way to the telephone, 'But I'm not at all sure it's Wednesday,' and his face fell.

Like most young children he loved any and all stores; unlike most, he created appalling scenes when he could not have everything that took his fancy. His range was not limited to candy and toys; he also wanted leashes, brightly coloured mixing bowls, ornaments for goldfish tanks. As Eve could not leave him at home while she shopped, and it was certainly not safe to lock him in the car, she had finally informed him with sternness that it was against the law in New Mexico for children to buy things in stores except on Wednesdays.

After a single bald exchange of 'Why?' and 'Don't ask *me*,' Ambrose accepted this, and although Eve supposed that she ought to worry about what it was doing to his psyche, if indeed he had one, she did not. The whole arrangement worked like a charm, because Wednesdays could be summoned or skipped at will. Ambrose enjoyed his small presents far more, Eve shopped in peace, everybody benefited.

She said now, when the other woman's voice came on the line, 'Sorry, Nina, there was someone here on the brink of leaving at last and I wanted to get the goodbyes done.' Better not mention the deputy and his errand; Nina seemed protective towards Henry Conlon and might decide to keep her own counsel. And certainly not, at this juncture, brace her about having been engineered into Conlon's orbit. 'You were saying, about the school—?'

'Yes, that I happened to remember that I know someone who did the layouts for the brochures when the place first opened, and I thought he might have kept track. It's pretty much what I thought. The fees were stiff and they went overboard on the proper-young-lady business. Even the parents were getting rebellious. It's since been turned into a very plush rest home if you ever feel like cracking up.'

'Thanks, I'll keep it in mind,' said Eve. She didn't know quite what she had expected when she dialed, but it was not this. 'Really just another failed enterprise.'

'So it would seem. Of course, mind you, it didn't help—' There was an odd sound here, some kind of flurry, and 'Damnation, I just knocked over my coffee. Hold on a second.'

Eve waited, listening to a distant shifting of objects, someone offering paper towels and advice about trying cold water first. Nina came back and said crossly, 'How can one stingy little paper cup hold a full gallon? But you don't *care* about my new avocado suit. It didn't help, I was starting to say, that one of the housemothers committed suicide.'

CHAPTER
FOURTEEN

Suicide. How black and suggestive that sounded, under the circumstances: a fatal leap, for instance, that was really a violent push . . . Briskly, somewhat dryly, Nina Earl dispelled any such picture.

Her friend the artist had apparently dug deep. The housemother, an unmarried fiftyish woman who came originally from Canada, had been suffering from periods of depression; both her doctor and her colleagues testified to this. It was believed that she had financial worries and had begun to fear dismissal from the school, but this was not definitely established because her discarded starts on a To Whom It May Concern note did not go far enough. Neat to the last, she had crumpled these into a wastebasket and then taken an overdose of barbiturates, incontrovertibly by her own hand.

'Even so, not the best example for the young ladies, and I don't suppose the parents liked it much,' Nina said in a judicial tone, 'but it certainly didn't close up the school. That lasted another year, into 1952, and then what finished it was something else entirely, some fuss about the land. And I don't see how Henry could have had the remotest connection with the place.'

The usually well-informed Nina was clearly unaware that at this moment the Sheriff's office was anxious to locate Conlon, and Eve did not enlighten her. She began, 'Thanks a lot—' and Nina

said aggrievedly, 'I had to have lunch with Al
Wasek to dig all this up, and he only eats at health
bars. The least you can do is tell me what's going
on.'

But at that point a background murmur of voices
grew; a layout was apparently missing and Eve was
delivered. She said, 'Later,' to Ambrose's impor-
tunate demands to find out if it was Wednesday,
and made herself another cup of coffee.

Henry Conlon had not been connected with the
Lockwood School; just as obviously, Jennifer
Morley had. The anonymous letter Mrs Morley had
brought him must have had its original basis there,
to judge from his reaction—and yet the suicide of
the housemother had to have been just that,
because surely the authorities would have been
especially meticulous under the circumstances.

It seemed unlikely that Jennifer had been a
student at the school as late as 1951. Her sister,
then, Mrs Pulliam? But, 'I barely knew Molly,'
Henry Conlon had said. And both of them were
dead, no longer concerned with anonymous letters
or anything else.

Eve jumped up and went to the little calendar on
her desk. (She must, she would break out of this
clinging web her mind was spinning, almost as
stickily tangible as some frightful fabrication from
the tool shed.) Gravely, and because it was part of
the ritual, she inspected September, which she had
forgotten to dispose of, and said to Ambrose's upturned face, red with hope and suspense, 'Let's go
and get you dressed, because it is Wednesday after
all'. . .'

Henry Conlon, who had not been in Colorado
where Eve's imagination placed him, was turning

away from a woman with startling green eye make-up and steady, competent hands. A typewriter clacked, an occasional figure passed by the windows, industriously busy about the manicured lawn and flower beds. He said, 'Thanks very much. I was sure anyway, after telephoning, but it was one of those things. I can find my way out.'

The woman smiled at him, a wry attractive smile. 'Just be sure you don't find your way *in*,' she said.

The Sheriff was on his way back from Colorado, having drawn a complete blank. A teletype to his opposite number there had assured him that there was nothing officially on the Vane family; he had hoped that, in a smallish community, there might be something unofficial.

If there was, it was buried too deep for recovery. Rufus Vane, dead for the past six years, had been a mild, widely liked, highly ineffectual rancher. His wife had died when a cloudburst swept her small car down an arroyo, leaving him with two daughters. Jennifer, the elder by five years, had more or less brought up Molly, taking a secretarial course after high school and going to work to help pad out the family finances. This was especially necessary after Vane had suffered a heart attack, making him incapable of keeping even an erring hand on the ranch.

Jennifer was remembered with respect and a liking tinged with caution. 'No nonsense about that one—well, it stands to reason. Molly was always a gay little thing, pretty as a buttercup, but Jennifer had the responsibilities and she showed it. When that swank school opened up here, years ago, she got a job in the office and helped put Molly through. She got engaged around that time but she

wouldn't have the wedding until her sister gradu-
ated. You have to hand it to her.'

You had to hand it to the whole family, the
Sheriff reflected sourly. No escapades, no scandal,
not so much as a parking ticket among the bunch of
them. Even the published accounts of the sisters'
deaths by violence had waked no spiteful reminis-
cences in a community which had known them well,
no voice to say, as so often happened, 'Well, I'm
not entirely surprised . . .'

It was nice to know that people could live such
open and blameless lives, but it was not helpful.
Even the school to the north where Jennifer had
worked to help with her sister's tuition had gone out
of existence, but Molly's prowess as a student and
Jennifer's ability with a typewriter could hardly
enter in.

Were they looking for a nut, then? A psychopath
with a fancied grudge? You had only to read the
newspapers to know that such people existed,
wearing the skins and the outward demeanour of
normal citizens, but their grudges seemed to be
against all humanity, their pressured, bottled-up
illness to explode upon living targets who simply
happened to be in the same place at the same time.
The seeking-out of two sisters, a week apart, did
not appear to fall in that category at all.

In this frame of mind, the Sheriff was all the more
pleased at the report waiting for him.

Arthur Pulliam had spent a large part of the
morning making funeral arrangements, as his
brother-in-law hardly seemed to know what he was
doing; his dazedness was like an alcoholic trance.
He said to all of Arthur's proposals, 'Whatever you
think,' or, docilely, 'Yes, that's probably best.'

Once he said with a terrible intentness—Richard, who would once have bitten his tongue through before confiding anything of an intimately personal nature to Arthur Pulliam—'We'd had a rough few days, you know, Jen and I, but that was all over and everything was fine.'

'For God's sake, don't go telling that to the police,' said Arthur alarmedly, but Richard was already back in his own driven world. Staring through Arthur, he said, 'I'm going to see that girl again. It's inconceivable that she could have been on the telephone and still not have the slightest inkling—'

But Jennifer could not have transmitted information which she herself did not possess, and they had proved that last night. Even if the murderer had passed boldly by the window of the room where she was telephoning, she would have heard but not seen him.

The room itself was tiny, hardly bigger than a spacious closet. The curtains at the single shoulder-high window did not meet, but on the wall directly opposite hung an oil abstract presented to the Morleys long ago by a friend and showing a really striking lack of talent. When the room was lighted, the uncurtained glass was painted impenetrably with silver and orange daisies, one impaled on a church steeple.

But going to see Miss Quinn was something active for Richard to do, and Arthur patted him on the shoulder and escaped to his office. He was himself shocked at the loss of his sister-in-law, but rather in the sense of the relict who had been overheard to say at the side of the ornate casket, 'You know, somehow I never liked her.'

Mr Heatherwood, wearing a bow tie which made him look like a voodoo doll, was at first dubious about the propriety of Arthur's return to his duties, but his triumph at having ousted the previous vice-president was even stronger. 'Perhaps work is best,' he said, and added with only a faint hint of menace, 'I trust that this whole sad business will be cleared up very soon. For your sake, my boy.'

Arthur cleaned out his files, with the newly hushed and respectful assistance of Miss Haines, and tried not to start at every ring of the telephone: surely this second tragedy would silence even Rosalinda, for the time being at least. Apparently it had. At four-thirty, the consensus being that it was unseemly for a man with a new bereavement in the family to finish out a full afternoon, he left the building and walked to the employees' parking lot. There, without warning, he came face to face with Rosalinda's stepfather.

Seen from a distance the man had looked to be a hulking brute; close up, he was even more so, with bronzed and pitted skin and a big curved nose as fierce as a scimitar. His stained white coveralls, his contemptuously leaning stance against the fender of Arthur's car, the fact that he had not shaved very recently combined to add inches and pounds. He said with open belligerence, 'You Pulliam?'

'I'm Mr Pulliam, yes.' The guard in his booth a hundred feet away—and how extremely distant that seemed at this moment—must have obligingly identified the car. Arthur made himself busy with his keys, and said with a bold attempt at nonrecognition, 'If you were looking for the employment office, it's two blocks west and south. You just turn at the—'

'You been fooling around with my daughter,' said Lopez baldly.

'I—well, really, sir! It's possible that your daughter may have been employed by us in some capacity,' began Arthur over a terrible inner quaking—and then, his senses sharpened by dread, because this looked like a man who would not only attempt physical violence but be quite successful at it, he realised that Lopez had not made the pronouncement threateningly; it had been more in the nature of a remark.

His relief that he was not to be the object of a beating died at once under the concurrent realisation that here it came at last: the demand for terms. Arthur felt none of the calm which is reputed to come when a long-feared threat turns into actuality, perhaps because he had been badly shaken by the deputy's attitude that morning. The deference and wholehearted sympathy of a week before had vanished; although the man had been polite enough he had been openly speculative. And for Arthur's association with Rosalinda Lopez to come out now, and be brandished about the newspapers . . . The first and possibly the least effect would be the immediate loss of his job here. He hardly dared think beyond that.

Lopez had brushed aside the flustered attempt at a disclaimer with a contemptuous slicing gesture with the edge of his hand. 'So what are you going to do about it?'

. . . *But*, Arthur was thinking frantically, neither Lopez nor Rosalinda could know of Mr Heatherwood's almost maniacal concern with morality, and they did know that he had been in Denver when Molly was killed. Might they accept a bluff: 'Very well, if you don't care about Rosalinda's reputation, go ahead, tell the police'? To gain time, he gazed at Lopez with an appearance of puzzlement and said, 'Do about what?'

Lopez stared back, baffled, beginning to scowl. 'My girl. Rosie.'

There ought to have been some faint comfort in hearing the haughty Rosalinda thus reduced, but there was not. Arthur's damp face felt cold in the little wind which had sprung up and was chasing spirals of dust around the parking lot. He was acutely conscious of the passing minutes which might bring a privileged few out of the building a little early, and of the fact that the guard at the gate, having nothing else to do, was almost certainly studying this menacing confrontation of a Heatherwood executive by a swarthy workman—because by now Lopez had placed his fists on his hips in an unmistakable attitude.

He must get himself out of here as quickly as possible without making any damaging admissions or concessions. Arthur began with all the austerity he could muster, 'If your daughter has any complaint as to her treatment here, she is free to make it through the proper channels. It's true that her employment here was abruptly terminated'—after that first date Arthur had swiftly found her another job—'and so it might be possible to arrange something by way of compensation. But now you really must excuse me, Mr Lopez, as I'm already late for an important—'

'Look,' interrupted Lopez, suddenly open and blunt. 'Rosie could make a lot of trouble for you—I read the papers, you know. Now, I got a brother in Vegas could get her a job there, she hates this dump anyway, and I figure maybe a thousand would get her some new clothes and expenses. Once she gets a look at Vegas she'll forget you ever existed, man.'

Two weeks ago Arthur would have been horrified at parting with such a sum unless it brought him something tangible and handsome. Now he wondered incredulously if for a mere thousand dollars he could be rid forever of this terrible threat to his job, his community standing, his very way of life? There must be a catch in it, unless for reasons of his own—Rosalinda had spoken with venom of her stepfather—Lopez was anxious to bundle her out of the way as speedily as possible and did not want to risk asking a larger demand.

Because the man had an air of sincerity, almost of appeal. He still looked dangerous when his brow clouded, but that might be an accident of feature: there were faces that could bring ferocity to a bowl of cornflakes. Arthur said guardedly that a thousand dollars was a great deal of money and that he would have to think about it. In the end—he was not quite sure how, but at any minute employees would begin to siphon into the parking lot—he was persuaded to part with a twenty- and a ten-dollar bill.

To a prejudiced and careful watcher there was something unmistakable about the transfer of money between two unlikely parties—the bent heads, the outcoming hand before the shielding turn of both bodies. The guard in his booth noted it, just as he had noted earlier the strange workman's bellicose stance, and the fact that he had been blocking the door of Mr Pulliam's car even though once or twice Mr Pulliam had appeared quite anxious to get into it.

The guard had no particular love for Pulliam, who tipped him scantily every Christmas with the air of bestowing a retirement fund. As soon as he was off duty, he telephoned and reported to his niece's husband, the deputy.

Eve Quinn was still shaken by a double encounter. Understandably, the identification at last of Ambrose's rockles was not accompanied by a slow, beginning roll of drums.

CHAPTER
FIFTEEN

'. . . No,' said Eve to Richard Morley's quietly pleading question. 'I've thought and thought about it, and there was absolutely nothing else at all.'

'Maybe that's it, maybe you've been concentrating too hard,' said Richard, producing this as eagerly as though it were a fresh concept. 'If you try and think of it as any ordinary phone call . . .'

Eve knew her limitations in this respect but she was enormously sorry for Richard, who would soon be attending another funeral, and she removed her glance to the fire she had lit in the arched adobe fireplace and sent her mind back obediently.

But there was nothing to remember in that interval after Mrs Morley had walked audibly away. On that rainy night it would have been an elementary precaution for the killer to remove his shoes before entering the house; still, it was an especially frightful detail, a kind of travesty of neatness and domesticity . . . Eve, who had been gazing into the gold wrap of the flames, found herself gazing instead at Richard Morley's calf-moccasined feet, and was suddenly so electrified with fear that she jerked back into the corner of the couch.

But nothing had happened; in his urgency he had only come to the edge of his chair at the exact instant when the wind sent a tree shadow rushing across the floor. But the impression of physical movement in the room, of a checked spring, was so strong that Eve jumped up at once, saying randomly, 'Excuse me a minute, I'd better see what Ambrose is doing—'

Ambrose, in accordance with the helpful instructions on a preschool television programme, was making a great gluey mass of papier-mâché in the bathroom sink. Apart from a fleeting wish that she could get her hands on the beaming, nodding originator of this suggestion, Eve did not mind at all. She said in a firm, carrying voice (to remind Richard Morley that she was not alone in this house, although she knew herself to be ridiculous), 'No more newspaper, Ambrose, and no more water. Don't you want to come in and say hello to Mr Morley?'

'I have to make this,' said Ambrose in an absorbed and silky voice. 'I have to make it.'

'Yes, I see that,' said Eve, as polite as he, and left him. Naturally Richard Morley had been watching her with that terrible attentiveness; he had hoped, not feared, that she would remember some tiny flaw in that stillness. He was distraught with grief and anger, and had a right to his— devouring look; he saw people now as mere tools for discovery.

(And the man who had struck down the two sisters: how did he look?)

In the living room, Richard seemed not to have noticed Eve's precipitate air; seemed, in fact, to have forgotten what they were talking about. He said abruptly, 'My wife didn't happen to mention anything about a letter, did she?'

'No, she didn't,' said Eve, but her heart lifted a little; this much of what Henry Conlon had told her about the other evening was true.

'Well, she got a letter that upset her, or frightened her, a few days ago. I don't know what it was about, or what became of it, and I don't think the police believe it ever existed at all,' said Richard with an air of mild wonder rather than bitterness, 'but it occurred to me that the sender might have been the one who came to the door.'

For some reason, this delineation was infinitely more chilling than 'murderer'; it carried the suggestion of violence knocking randomly, not caring particularly who answered. And at that instant, as though on signal, a car door slammed in the driveway.

Richard Morley, who had been about to leave, walked back into the living room and stared out through one of the tall windows. Eve, watching his face, saw for the first time why Jennifer might have kept a worrying secret from her husband. He said in a tight, hard voice, 'Well, if it isn't the old friend from Colorado,' remembered at the door to thank Eve perfunctorily, and was gone.

'I thought I'd assure you that I've just been to the Sheriff's office and accounted satisfactorily for my whereabouts last night,' said Henry Conlon to Eve in a brisk recitative tone. He added reflectively, 'Under the circumstances, I'm surprised that you let me in just now.'

Eve, who for a confused moment thought he meant his thunderclap departure of the night before, gazed at the wrist he held out, the wrist with the long scratch.

'I'd forgotten I had it. Luckily, Mrs Birchall remembered.'

Mrs Birchall, Henry explained, lived in his apartment building and had a small enterprising daughter named Flora whom she was in the habit of taking to the park across the street. Mrs Birchall was also a great reader, and read indefatigably while Flora fell into the fountain or started into the traffic and was rescued by whoever happened to be handy. Late on the afternoon of the day before, Flora had managed to attain a perilous height in a tree and it had fallen to Henry's lot to climb up after her and thereby come into conflict with a branch.

'It's a wonder that Mrs Birchall noticed the scratch at all. Usually she just says, "I'm surprised at you, Flora" and goes back to her book.' The faint amusement died out of Henry's face. 'I met Morley outside. We had a few words, to put it mildly. He said he found it hard to believe that I had been living here and hadn't attempted to get in touch with my, quote, "old friend" until so recently. I said I found it worse than hard to believe that he could think his wife had a male friend who was anything more than that. It was not,' said Henry ruefully, 'a very edifying conversation.'

The fire had died down to an occasional brilliant blink and a simmer. Eve added another small piñon log and said with a careful lack of expression, 'He seemed to think that whoever wrote his wife that letter might have killed her.'

'No.' The denial came out with complete certainty. 'That's a total, physical impossibility. Beside which it has no bearing on all this, on what happened to Jennifer or her sister. It was an entirely separate thing, and it was only Jennifer's emotional state—'

Henry broke off there, in a kind of baffled way. He said soberly, holding Eve's gaze with gravity, 'If anybody ever offers you a choice between a confidence to respect or a tiger that hasn't eaten in six months, take the tiger. It'll make better company.'

There seemed no answer to that, and obviously he did not expect one. After a roaming glance about him he asked, 'Do you think you're safe here?'

The question didn't startle Eve; she had already considered it. 'I don't know why not. The newspapers only said that Mrs Morley had been on the phone with a friend, and obviously a friend who knew anything incriminating would have told the police right away.'

'And where's the guarantee that you won't remember something? Richard Morley knows that you were talking to his wife, and he's certainly told his brother-in-law, and they've probably both told other people.'

'You can't remember something that didn't happen,' said Eve, 'and although I can't tell you why, exactly, I'm sure that whoever hung up that phone knows he's safe from me.'

(Forget that not half an hour ago she had fled this room, terrified by a trick of the wind, governed by instinct and not by logic or reason. Henry Conlon was now regarding her with something of the same attention, but she did not feel the slightest tinge of fear.)

A chilly grey bloom was coming over the afternoon, and there was a beginning brush of wind around the house. As naturally as though he lived there, and would presently get up and fix drinks, Henry stretched out his hand and switched on the lamp beside him. His hand stayed there, arrested in the odd intimacy of the gesture, and his glance held Eve's for a long moment that left her feeling a little light-headed, or enclosed in a bubble. 'If you need any papier-mâché,' she said inanely, 'Ambrose is whipping up some in the bathroom.'

'You were better off with the horned toad,' said Henry, matching her mood with accuracy. 'Some day we must introduce Ambrose to Flora.' He rose and moved towards the door, frowning abstractedly. 'I think I'll sleep next door tonight,' he said.

It was nearly full dark before Eve remembered the old pillow slip she had hung out on the line that morning, and she only remembered it then as a possible distraction for Ambrose, who had slipped and fallen on a sodden ribbon of newspaper half an hour ago and was still sobbing reminiscently. 'Good Lord, I hope nobody took your cloth,' she said with an air of alarm, and let herself out the back door.

She had often been outside here at night, usually to get something forgotten in the car, but she had never noticed before how far short of the clothesline the block of radiance from the kitchen fell, or the peculiar pattern of branch shadows on the adobe wall along the road. When the cottonwood leaves rattled overhead, the shadows seemed to take on life and pour over the wall like slender animals on a secret invasion. Eve, who had approached the clothesline at a sensible pace, unpinned the pillow slip in darkness and ran back to the house at almost panic speed.

Ambrose examined the cloth with great care and, finally, satisfaction. 'No germs,' he said, turning his still-red and tear-streaked face up to Eve.

'Of course not.' Was he going to start that again?

'Saxon said germs. Dreadly germs.'

'Mrs Saxon.' Eve felt a trace of annoyance at Iris, who should know by now that Ambrose, with his anxious and loving regard for his own person, was the last child who needed lectures of that nature.

'Saxon,' corrected Ambrose firmly, 'and he *took* my rockles.' He put the pillow slip in Eve's lap and clambered up on the arm of the couch, breathing heavily and moistly in her ear. 'Now cut it, in a tringe.'

Eve let that go by; tringe was close enough. As she went in search of her scissors she reflected that she must be the only rockles-maker in existence, because it was a certainty that when she had finished fringing the cloth Ambrose would demand that she sew on a coloured patch. She was less surprised by the identification of the missing treasure (was it the pocketlike appearance of the other patch that had suggested that peculiar name?) than by Ambrose's firm conviction that Ned Saxon had deprived him of it.

And the tool shed was tied up in it somewhere, or so he thought. Eve recalled the afternoon, an impossible length of time ago, when Ambrose had tugged imperiously at her hand and led her towards the shed. He had stopped short then, as though some memory had frightened him, and Eve, not wanting to enter the place herself, had said, 'You can't possibly have left anything of yours in there.'

She supposed now that he could have slipped inside behind someone—for all his plumpness and his ability to trip on perfectly flat surfaces he was surprisingly fast—but even granted that he had dropped the cloth in the shed, what would Ned Saxon, or indeed anybody else, want with it? It might have been used to wipe oily hands, of course, or clean a windshield, and no one but Ambrose would recognise it as being of inestimable value . . . better not pursue the matter, as there was no great love between Ambrose and the Saxons as it was. Besides—Eve was now cutting an oblong out of a printed blouse she had never liked—it wasn't important, as she was almost finished with the substitute.

Because she thought of the tool shed in terms of spiders and shadows and even possibly snakes, Eve had forgotten its primary purpose. No picture presented itself of a man selecting a hammer which could hardly be traced to him, stowing it in a pocket, realising from a sound behind him that he had a three-year-old watcher. Diverting the child's attention while he snatched up a rag from the floor and wrapped it concealingly around the shaft of the hammer, saying later to the indignant and accusing Ambrose, 'That old piece of cloth? You didn't want that, it had deadly germs on it . . .'

An enticing oven scent emerged from the kitchen. 'Dinner's ready,' said Eve.

Iris Saxon was also preparing dinner in an abstracted way, her face pale and frowning with thought. From bewilderment, she had slipped without any conscious process into at least a sharing of

Ned's cool assessment of Arthur Pulliam. 'But I don't see *why*. It seems so . . . I don't know, impossible.'

'I don't see why either,' said Ned Saxon, 'but he was certainly acting very odd that day.' His brilliant blue gaze, wrinkled at the corners, might have been that of a captain staring at a periscope where no submarine is supposed to be—but this was a very friendly submarine. 'You'll admit that he forced that drink on us, all of a sudden.'

'Well, he did seem very jumpy,' admitted Iris, adding a tiny sprinkle of salt to the boiled squash, but no pepper; Ned's stomach could not tolerate spices. 'But you know that Jennifer was never crazy about Arthur, and even she never thought for a minute that he had anything to do with what happened to Molly. If she'd had the slightest suspicion . . .'

'Maybe she found out something the day she was there at the house,' suggested Ned softly. 'You never know about people, Iris. Maybe Arthur Pulliam looks like a church deacon just because he isn't anything like a church deacon, underneath.'

A year ago, Iris would have refuted this. Now she said uncertainly, 'Well, he did take a lot of trips away . . .'

'And if murderers looked like murderers there wouldn't be any crime rate, would there? Your trouble is that you believe the best of everybody,' said Ned Saxon fondly.

He ate his dinner with appetite, agreeing with Iris that the cheaper grade of hamburger had more flavour; this was a long-established ritual. As always, he insisted on doing the dishes—there could scarcely have been a more thoughtful husband—and he was polishing glasses with his usual careful attention when the telephone rang.

That was an item soon to be pruned from their budget, thought Ned with ferocious pleasure, and Iris, who was closer, answered it. After listening for a few moments she said, 'I don't know, hon—just let me ask Ned,' and covered the mouthpiece. 'Eve Quinn wants to know if I can give her an extra day tomorrow. The little boy's father is going to pick him up some time this week and she wants to get his clothes—'

Ned Saxon shook his head. 'No.' It was fortunate that he was holding a jelly glass with the label carefully scrubbed off; anything thinner would have smashed under the sudden furious pressure of his fingers. 'It's just too much for you right now.'

Iris uncovered the mouthpiece again, obediently. 'Eve? I'm awfully sorry, but Ned doesn't think—'

The courteous feminine exchanges went on for another minute or so. Controlledly, his back turned at the sink, Ned sponged the tiny counter, closed a cupboard door. There was no one to see the dangerous clenched look of his face, a vein beating at the temple with rage; no one, even seeing, could have guessed at the thoughts churning inside: *Charity*. Have pity on your poor servants, the Saxons, and manufacture an extra day's work for Iris. Surely you can scrape up enough laundry and ironing, if you look hard enough, and then you can write out a check, Lady Bountiful Quinn, there's not much labour in that . . .

But he had spoken too sharply in his refusal, because Iris's face as she hung up wore a surprise and questioning expression, along with something else which Ned determinedly did not recognise as disappointment. 'You know all this has been a great shock to you,' he said in a mild and reasonable tone. 'You haven't even been sleeping properly. Your health has to be the first consideration . . .'

The Saxons owned a television set with a faulty tube that often bent the performers on the screen into astonishing arcs and ellipses, and they watched it every evening with the gravity and unselectivity of children. Ned took his usual chair tonight, but although his ruddy face looked attentive the attention was all inward.

For a man armoured only by his own devouring hatred, he had already been given two surprising assists by Providence. In the case of Molly Pulliam, there had been the unlooked-for diversion of the yardman; in the case of Jennifer Morley there was the undoubted fact that she had spent several hours alone in her brother-in-law's house and he was very nervous about something.

The disposal of Eve Quinn, the final erasure of the face-in-the-dirt humiliation, had presented a more delicate problem, ruling out as it would the generally accepted theory that the two women had died because they were sisters, victims of someone from their common background. Even in the depths of his obsession Ned Saxon realised that with the death of Eve Quinn it would be pointed out that there was a common denominator in all these households.

But Eve Quinn had obligingly been on that open line in the Morley house, and although Ned was quite sure that he had approached the phone without sound it would be natural for the police to assume that the Quinn girl had died because she possessed dangerous knowledge.

. . . He would begin laying the groundwork for that very soon.

CHAPTER
SIXTEEN

In view of the headlines and the columns of type, a sombre editorial and a cruel inset of her face in a blurry photograph of the rain-wet outdoor fireplace, there were surprisingly few people at Jennifer Morley's funeral.

A selection of Richard's broker colleagues came, looking like gangsters turned respectable for the day in identical dark suits, and a bare scattering of friends; the vast number of flowers testified to the unease of the absent ones. The Saxons were there, seated firmly towards the back of the church—no one was going to have the opportunity of ushering them out of choicer pews—and a handful of obvious sensation-seekers who stared at the rigid backs of Richard Morley and his brother-in-law and whispered among themselves. The air over the large stretch of empty pews seemed thick with embarrassment and defensiveness. It was a little like the funeral of someone who had died of a terrible and infectious disease.

Neither the Pulliams nor the Morleys had thought of needing plots so soon, and as a result Jennifer was buried on the far side of the cemetery. It was a windy day, the sunlight with a jewelled coldness and brightness, and when the cedar branches shifted a little it was possible to see, in the distance, a few dim touches of colour on that other, earlier grave. Everybody in the small group now whittled down to the two bereaved husbands, the Saxons, and a couple named Harkness, was careful not to look—everybody except Ned Saxon, who lifted his orange head just before they all turned away and sent a long look across the grass.

Some of this Eve learned from Henry Conlon, who had been quietly at the church but did not test Richard Morley's control by proceeding to the cemetery. She herself had been unabashedly relieved that there was no one to stay with Ambrose and therefore no possibility of her own attendance. She had sent flowers.

She would have been shocked by Ned Saxon's savage appraisal of her motives in asking Iris for an extra day's help, the more so because it came very close to the truth.

Her cousin Celia had called from New York, as arranged. With the memory of her own seizure of pure fright out at the clothesline in the dark, while the night rustled slyly around her, Eve had made up her mind that she would—without frightening Celia out of her wits—ask that Roger fly out and collect Ambrose. She did not seriously think of leaving the little house, but she knew that she would have more freedom of action, and far less concern, if she were alone and unencumbered.

Celia's first words undid all that. 'Eve? How are you? We've been half out of our minds here. Thank God you've got Ambrose—do you think you could stand him just a little longer? Roger's mother had a bad stroke on Thursday, and the doctor is afraid that if we try to move her to a hospital right now— you know what she's like . . .' In her agitation Celia had obviously forgotten that Eve had never laid eyes on Roger's mother. Eve gazed aghast at her kitchen wall, seeing her own plan vanishing like water down a drain.

'. . . nurse with her, in our room, of course,' Celia was saying distractedly, 'and I'm in *her* room, and poor Roger's on the couch, and of course everything has to be absolutely quiet.' Her voice did indeed have a harried, hunted sound, as if the nurse might appear at any moment with a finger at her lips. 'So if you could possibly keep Ambrose for a few more days, until we get things better arranged here—'

Eve said of course, because there was no alternative; inquired about Celia's back, reported on Ambrose, and presently hung up. She did not immediately leave the telephone, because as she talked her glance had fallen on one of Iris Saxon's meticulous notations of things to be bought for the house: cinnamon, distilled water for the iron, detergent. She had written that on her last day here, when in answer to Eve's parting thanks she had replied cheerfully, 'It's even nicer that we can eat.'

What would the Saxons do now, in the interim period before Ned Saxon found work or they supplemented their income in some other way? Eve knew that they were painfully poor and always a few bills behind; she also knew that here in the Southwest, perhaps even more than elsewhere, employment of any kind was hard to come by for people nearing sixty. Iris's weekly thirty-six dollars had enabled them to eke out an existence, and that had dwindled to twelve. It seemed shocking to relate the deaths of two women in terms of financial loss, but the loss was certainly there.

Impulsively, Eve lifted the receiver again and dialed. She was not in a position to offer much help, or not over a long period of time, but suppose that right now some immediate creditor were pressing for even a token payment?

She told Iris about Ambrose's coming departure—true in a sense, because surely they were not going to grow old together?—and waited. When Ned Saxon's opinion was relayed she could feel her face flood warmly even though she was alone and unobserved. 'Oh, of course. I should have—'

'I'm all right really, it's just delayed reaction, I guess. Or maybe old age creeping up,' said Iris, pitiably gay. This was a subject she raised with defiant frequency, as though to befriend the advancing years and perhaps lessen their toll. 'When did you say they were coming for the little boy?'

'Before the end of the week.' All Eve wanted now was to be released from the peculiar humiliation she had brought on her own head, but she was not to be let go so easily. Iris discussed dates anxiously and it was finally settled that she would come a day earlier than usual. 'But only if you really feel up to it,' said Eve, and was free at last.

How, knowing the Saxons' polite but iron pride, had she let herself in for such a well-deserved rebuff? It was a pity that a telephone call could not be left overnight in its actuality, like a letter which you might regard with fresh eyes in the morning . . .

Henry Conlon had kept to his plan; as she poured herself a cup of coffee Eve could see the lights in the other house glowing. Comforted but at the same time reminded, she checked all the locks before she gathered her book and cigarettes, switched off the living room lamps, and went in to look at Ambrose. After all her cutting and sewing he had had, like most children presented with a substitute, no use at all for the artfully fringed and patched cloth; he had simply handed it back to Eve as though it were something of hers. The straw hat had also fallen from favour and lay unregarded on the floor, but even in sleep Ambrose had a firm grip on the spark plug.

Eve was presently asleep herself, her dreams pricked through now and then by the crisp sleety rustle of fallen leaves around the little house. It had not crossed her mind, troubled as she was by her own tactlessness, that she had received not so much a rebuff as a sharp stinging slap from a hand aching to deliver it.

Two days after Jennifer Morley's funeral, the elderly proprietor of a small candy store in the Heights was struck down and robbed only minutes after she had opened the place for business. There were no eyewitnesses, and the victim died of head injuries a few hours later without regaining consciousness.

Although apart from the common sex involved there was no resemblance between this crime and the Valley murders, an immediate if unstated connection was made in the public mind by the new black headlines, the fresh Page One photographs. The Sheriff had a hasty conference with the city police chief, because while to anyone reading the daily burglary reports it might seem unlikely that there was a single private home in Albuquerque retaining its typewriter or television set, crimes of violence were by no means that common.

The city police were more fortunate than the Sheriff in having what seemed to be a large jump on their man. Shortly before dawn they had received an emergency call from an apartment eight blocks away from the candy store where, as the result of an all-night drinking party, a youth had been stabbed. The assailant had fled, but one of the two sullen but terrified girls present at these festivities had furnished a description although she could not provide the man's name. ('Probably telling the truth at that,' remarked the chief grimly.) It was a matter of hours later when a stolen-car complaint came in from the same neighbourhood; the complainant said in a confused fashion that he hadn't reported it earlier because he had assumed that his brother-in-law had borrowed it again. 'Anything you don't nail down that kid takes—except his sister.'

All of this might fit together as tidily as they would like: on the other hand, the knifing and the stolen car might be fragments that had touched accidentally and would fly off in different directions. As a result, the close of the newspaper account said only that road blocks had been set up.

Ned Saxon read the story through that evening and then, with greater care, read it again. A lamp might have been lit behind his highly coloured features, lending them a look almost of exaltation. In his mind he sifted and weighed the phrases: 'Brutality of the blows . . . taken by surprise . . . tenant in the apartment above heard no outcry.'

He let the paper drop to his knees, and did not know that he had said aloud in a soft and wondering voice, 'That's the third time.'

Iris Saxon, preoccupied with the worries that she never let him see, often allowed these commentaries on the evening paper to go by with only an absent 'Hmm?' because usually they concerned paving regulations or reapportionment or other matters which she felt vaguely belonged in the male domain. Tonight, caught by his tone, she turned from the stove to ask, 'Third time for what?'

Her back shivered tinily then, because Ned was gazing at her attentively and not seeing her at all. On the other hand he seemed so amazed, even in his blankness, that she put smoothing hands to her hair as though it had sprung on end to surprise him.

She realised almost at once that the oddity of his glance was caused by the low-watt bulbs they used for economy: somehow the strain of reading newsprint in that had made his richly blue eyes look unfamiliarly black. Ned obviously realised it at the same time, because he twisted in the chair with the groaning spring, tweaked the lampshade, and said quite briskly. 'Third holdup of a small independent business in—what is it?—less than a month. It goes to show you what enterprise amounts to, these days . . .'

This was familiar ground, and Iris agreed with everything he said and dealt out the stewed chicken backs and rice, the peas, an exact half of the jelly roll which would, in its remainder, serve them for breakfast.

The television set was more erratic than usual that night, with events apparently taking place inside a wicker basket, and although Ned said that he would stay up and watch the news, Iris went to bed. The fitful mutter about floor wax and France, Washington sources and fluorides, built up a kind of peaceful hum around her, like a protective skin. She slid into sleep, and it might have been the very cessation of sound that half woke her.

Was it an hour later, or more than that? Iris thought drowsily of asking Ned, but she did not want to bring herself completely awake. Besides, from the silence and the dimness of the ceiling, he was in the bathroom, from which he would presently emerge to turn off the solitary lamp.

He wasn't in the bathroom. When Iris turned over in bed to ease her stiff shoulder he was a bulky dark shape on his knees in front of the old armchair with the broken spring.

She watched him with the idle unreality of someone still partly bound by sleep, accepting his odd posture with a kind of mild interest. Quietly, absorbedly, he was pulling back the length of old blanket which, tucked tightly around the seat cushion, hid the torn upholstery and helped contain the broken spring. He was beginning to probe with his fingers when Iris, growing more alert with every second, asked curiously, 'What are you doing?'

Her voice sounded unnaturally loud in the secret, almost trancelike silence. Ned was totally, fleetingly still before his hand began to move again. He said without turning his head, 'I lost that good mechanical pencil you gave me and I thought it might have slipped down in here, but'—he retucked the blanket and rose cumbersomely to his feet—' I guess not. Oh, well, I'll look for it in the morning.'

He was spared the trouble. The door of the refrigerator was defective, and when Iris gave it the necessary slam the next morning there was a bounce and a metallic rattle as the pencil hit the floor. Ned inspected it for damage, pocketed it, and drove off for the morning paper, which he would peruse in the car; if there was anything promising in the Help Wanted column—they both clung sturdily to the fantasy that there might be—he would continue straight on and apply. If not, he would return home and work on some of the repairs the apartment always needed.

When he had gone, Iris dried and put away the few breakfast things. She refrained loyally from wishing that she were at Eve Quinn's pretty little house right now, chatting over a companionable second cup of coffee; she reminded herself that although Eve couldn't be nicer the child was terribly spoiled and had the removed, assessing gaze of a Siamese cat, which was bad enough in something with fur and four legs.

She also reminded herself that as Ned's pencil had been found there was no real reason to be bending over the old armchair, pulling the piece of blanket out of its tucking, thrusting her fingers in around the broken spring like a woman who must destroy a spider at once or else retreat from it with the knowledge that, later, it might scurry out of a magazine in her lap or hide in her sweater sleeve.

But there was nothing there, or nothing but stuffing and lint and the broken spring. Not knowing that she did it, certainly not knowing why, Iris Saxon closed her eyes momentarily and drew in a great breath. Anyone observing might have thought she had found, instead of the dilapidation inside an old chair, a handful of gold.

CHAPTER
SEVENTEEN

At odd moments of the day and in wakeful hours of the night, Arthur Pulliam took cautious little pulls at the thread which might unravel the nightmare spun about him.

'We're both men of the world, Sheriff,' he said rehearsingly to himself, and abandoned that at once. The Sheriff was firmly not a man of the world, and would be outraged at any imputation that he was.

'Frankly, Sheriff, I have a little confession to make—' But his Pulliam blood writhed at the word confession, and the Sheriff would certainly not consider adultery little.

Very well, then; what about a rueful 'I'm afraid I was badly taken in, Sheriff, by a young girl in my employ—tales of abuse at home, you know the kind of thing . . .' No. They had only to look at Rosalinda.

But if only there were a way to gain official protection against the Lopezes without bringing about the very exposure it was so essential to avoid. More than forty-eight hours of silence from that quarter had only increased Arthur's apprehension like mildew. He stepped without pleasure on the thicker carpeting in his new office, noted apathetically that he now had an extra button on his telephone, derived no consolation even from the glossy and formidable plant in its tub. Richardson, after all, had been evicted from the midst of these splendours because of a simple and discreet divorce.

The more Arthur thought about it, and he thought about little else, the stranger it was that Lopez had been allowed to set the terms for silence. Apart from a kind of reluctant admiration for the ferocity of his temper, Rosalinda had only contempt for her stepfather; it seemed very odd that she would let such a golden opportunity rest in his hands. Particularly as her manner at their last meeting had been both purring and mocking: the manner of a woman with some devastating stroke up her sleeve. Even in her peculiar simplicity, Rosalinda would not regard a thousand dollars as devastating.

For that matter, had there been something odd about Lopez himself, even apart from his amiability?

Arthur might have pursued that impression, might have felt the first loosening of the tangle, except for a sudden realisation that, occurring to him without warning in the middle of a meeting, turned him almost giddy with fright.

In his shock at being confronted by Lopez in the parking lot, he had noted the man's coveralls only in the sense that they made a more menacing garb than, say, a dark blue single-breasted suit. Now, out of nowhere, his mind supplied the coveralls with a faint clanking sound when Lopez moved, a wink of metal. Rosalinda's stepfather was a carpenter by trade, and the weapon that had killed Molly was, the report had said, something closely resembling a hammer.

From a great distance, Mr Heatherwood's voice said frigidly, 'We don't quite seem to have Arthur's attention here,' and Arthur collected himself and put a hand apologetically to his jaw. 'Sorry, sir. An ulcerated tooth—'

'Miss Molloy, bring two aspirins for Mr Pulliam, please. And a glass of water,' added Mr Heatherwood with the air of a man pandering to weakness, and the meeting went on.

A small portion of Arthur's mind knew, when he was safely back in his own office, that Lopez had certainly not murdered Molly—but how would it look to the police, who would be ready by this time to pounce on the slightest appearance of a lead? In the light of his involvement with Rosalinda, would they believe that Arthur had never wished his wife dead; would have been horrified at even the suggestion of a divorce? Or would they reason that he had procured Molly's death, and that Jennifer had somehow found it out?

Arthur shuddered at the thought that he had even contemplated confiding in the Sheriff, because the very investigation that would prove him innocent would also accomplish his effective ruin.

It was five o'clock at last, but he was doomed to a visit from Mr Heatherwood, who wanted to hear a little verbal appreciation of Arthur's new office and status and also to give him a lecture on the care of his teeth. 'We're soft, my boy,' he said, poking inquisitively with his cane at the earth around the huge potted plant to see if it had been properly watered. 'Rushing like lemmings to our own disaster on our diet of white bread and flesh meats and cooked vegetables. To say nothing of sweets. One might almost say that our teeth have grown sedentary.' Pleased with this, Mr Heatherwood repeated it before he went on, and on.

In his acute nervousness, one of Arthur's teeth had actually started to ache, something which could not have occurred in Mr Heatherwood's celery-grinding, carrot-champing dentures. He was released at last, and bought an evening paper from the newsboy in the parking lot. The headline announcing the apprehension of a suspect in the candy-store killing caught but did not hold his eye in view of a brief inset bulletin stating that the man in question had been reposing in a Flagstaff jail at the time of the Valley murders.

The guard in his booth, who had been such an attentive witness to the encounter with Lopez, usually nodded and touched his cap as Arthur Pulliam nosed his car through the gates. Tonight, instead, he gave Arthur a deliberate stare which seemed half challenge and half satisfaction, and, in the rearview mirror, could be seen to turn his head and watch the car out of sight.

A few days ago Arthur would have been affronted by this insolence. He realised now that he had just received a warning.

The Sheriff came to the Pulliam house that evening ostensibly to return the thick manila envelope of snapshots, letters, and other documents conscientiously gathered from Molly Pulliam's small desk and examined in the light of her sister's errand shortly before her death. But when the receipt had been signed he remained seated, in spite of Arthur's nudging, 'Can I offer you coffee, Sheriff? A drink?'

The Sheriff refused both. He remarked in a regretful way that Richard Morley had been subjected to some unpleasantness at his home—a

Spanish jar smashed, a swastika chalked on the front door.

'Kids, and we have a pretty good idea which ones. I have a man checking on that now. You haven't had any of that trouble?'

Arthur Pulliam shook his head. 'Should I expect it, Sheriff? Because when all this is—that is, in the near future I'll be putting this place on the market, and if you think it's advisable to have someone stay on the premises for the time being—'

'Oh, I don't think that's necessary, word will get around that we're keeping an eye out. But with all the publicity you haven't been bothered by any of the usual cranks who crop up in cases like this?'

There was something bordering upon a silence, and then Arthur Pulliam turned his head to give his finicky attention to a fold of curtain hanging not quite straight beside his chair. Light slid dazzlingly off his glasses as he turned back. 'It's interesting that you should ask that, because until just now it didn't occur to me—'

But it had occurred to him, thought the Sheriff, because he was quite smooth and ready with his account of a strange and belligerent workman—'The fellow had been drinking, I believe'—who had accosted him in the company parking lot and seemed to think he could have a job simply by demanding one. 'I have nothing to do with the hiring, and I told him so, but a man of his type, in that frame of mind—'

Pulliam spread his hands in a deprecating and half-humorous gesture which looked to the Sheriff completely alien. 'From what you say now, I suppose he'd read of my connection with the company, and to be honest he was a good deal bigger than I am. He kept going on about being a hardship case, and in order to get rid of him I gave him a couple of dollars.'

It was a lot of detail for a man of Pulliam's pompous nature to volunteer, and it countered the guard's report so suavely that he had clearly been braced for this. And, on the face of it, what more appropriate place for an out-of-work carpenter than a construction company? Except that these were Heatherwood's general offices and austerely uninviting to workmen in coveralls. Moreover, Arthur Pulliam gave the strong impression of having little sympathy with hardship cases, let alone drinking hardship cases—and the guard, to whom the carpenter had come to have Pulliam's car pointed out, had said nothing about any evidence of liquor.

Was it interesting that Pulliam should have been threatened by and given money to a man in that particular walk of life? The Sheriff was inclined to think so. 'As he was looking for a job, I suppose he gave you his name?'

'Yes, he did,' said Pulliam equably. 'I don't remember it, but it struck me at the time as being Italian or possibly Portuguese.'

So certainly neither, thought the Sheriff. He rose to his formidable height. 'Well, we like to look into these things. Maybe the guard at the gate will know the man.'

'Maybe he will,' agreed Pulliam, apparently recognising this possibility for the first time. 'Certainly I recall his glancing at us several times . . . You'll let me know, of course, the minute anything develops in this terrible business?'

'Yes,' said the Sheriff gently, angered at this

not-quite-open recognition of his empty threat. 'I will do that, Mr Pulliam.'

Something there, almost certainly, he thought, getting into his car in the cold darkness—and almost certainly not traceable; the guard had never seen the man in question before, and Pulliam would be quite safe in sticking to his version. If only, he thought for perhaps the thousandth time since taking office, he had more men—a man, for instance, to hold a watching brief on Arthur Pulliam. But routine crime went on in the Valley in spite of the two women so recently buried: gas stations and liquor stores were still held up, alcoholic spouses still turned on their mates with whatever damaging object came to hand, television sets and radios and other portables were burgled at a dizzy pace.

At the corner of the driveway the Sheriff met headlights turning in. He caught a brief glimpse of a woman's pale pointed face on the passenger side, and the outline of a man at the wheel. Under the circumstances he would have been interested in a lone woman's evening visit to Arthur Pulliam. He was not interested in a couple, and he drove broodingly away.

'Eve?' said Nina Earl's voice when Eve caught the telephone on its fifth ring. 'I know it's late, but my conscience keeps peculiar hours . . . did I wake you up?'

'If it were anyone else I'd say no,' said Eve, sleep-bewildered and cross. She pushed her hair back with her free hand and peered uselessly at the clock; in her present state she was unable to read it.

'Well, I told you about Al Wasek,' began Nina, maddeningly alert miles away. 'You know, the health-bar nut, the artist who did the layouts for the Lockwood School.'

Eve felt suddenly drenched awake. The clock hands steadied and showed only a few minutes after eleven—which was what came, she thought, of living with a small child. 'Yes, I remember.'

'Al's been reading the papers, of course, but the thing you have to keep in mind is that he's getting a divorce from his wife and custody of the children, he hopes, and has to walk on *eggs*, so whatever you do about this you can't mention him. Or me,' said Nina as a firm afterthought. 'You haven't gone back to sleep, have you?'

'No, just getting a cigarette.' Ridiculously, in view of her own earlier pursuit of this very matter, Eve felt a pang of dread because she was finally to learn about the Lockwood School—and that, of course, was the memory of Henry Conlon saying wryly, '. . . take the tiger. It'll make better company.'

And now the secret was out, in this random and accidental fashion—or was it? 'I don't know what if anything this has to do with those awful goings-on out there in the Valley. Nothing, I should think, but you did ask me about the school, and you did seem to have a bee in your bonnet about Henry, and I thought you ought to know that the housemother who committed suicide at the school was a cousin or something of Richard Morley's. There, I've done my duty and,' said Nina with magnificent unfairness, '*I'm* going to bed.'

CHAPTER
EIGHTEEN

The suicide again. And an echo of Richard Morley's taut, barely held control when he had sat on the couch questioning Eve . . .

'Was that Mommy?' asked Ambrose in the doorway, sleep-flushed and anxious. The pyjama legs that Eve had inexpertly turned up for him in Iris Saxon's absence had come down, indeed seemed to have grown somewhat, and lay in little striped puddles on the floor. It was the kind of thing that would normally have enraged him, but in his almost accusing concentration he only gave the bottoms an absent pluck and began again, 'Was that—'

'No, that wasn't your mother, it was just a friend of mine.' Surely he would not pick this hour of the night to get homesick. Yes, he would. 'I want to go home,' said Ambrose in a rising wail, and commenced to cry.

Eve had endured his tears of wrath with calm and even a measure of amusement; this was something else again, and as surprising, although it should not have been, as though a warlike dog had started to mew. She tried some helpless soothing, which made matters worse: Ambrose's face turned an alarming colour and his tears ran into the corners of his mouth. It was only when Eve said very crisply, 'Well, they have to make the airplane, don't they?' that a fascinated pause descended.

'Make the airplane,' repeated Ambrose.

'Yes. It's a big job.'

'With the wings.'

'Certainly, wings—I should hope so—and then they have to put on the tail, and a few other things. It takes a while.'

Ambrose was absorbed, and even twisted his tongue around to catch a few halted tears; clearly, some gratifying vision of people labouring solely on his behalf was taking place in his head. He was so pleased that he wanted to stay up and chat about it, but was presently persuaded to bed after a drink of water and a trip to the bathroom, from which he emerged saying with something of his old aplomb, 'I made a A.'

And so he had, with toothpaste on the inside of the sink. Partly out of her own fatigue, partly from a dim notion that he might find that straggly creation a talisman in the morning, Eve left it undisturbed. His emotional storm had been a blessing in a way; she was too tired to think about what Nina Earl had told her. Her last waking reflection was a hope that by morning Ambrose would have forgotten about going home, because morning would bring Iris Saxon.

Four miles away, Arthur Pulliam was not at all sleepy although it was long past his customary hour of retiring. If he had been a man given to pinching himself he would have been black-and-blue. As it was, he was filled with the balked exhilaration of someone who has just been given a clean bill of health by his doctor and cannot even tell anyone he has been ill.

He was sure, at the sound of a car in the drive less than a full minute after he had closed the front door, that the Sheriff had returned. Had he embroidered his encounter with Lopez too much? But the man, once reported, had had to be explained away somehow. Arthur opened the door with deliberate impatience, prepared to make some chilly protest at this harassment, and Rosalinda walked in.

The timing of this had so much the air of a planned confrontation that Arthur half-expected the Sheriff to follow, but the driver of the low unfamiliar car outside, its motor running softly, was a young man engaged in lighting a cigarette. 'Close the door, I have only a minute,' said Rosalinda, both waspish and breathless, and, caught between bewilderment and fright, Arthur closed it.

Rosalinda was wearing a loose ivory coat and a subtly different look, which might have been the sweeping of her black hair back and up from her face, emphasising the imperious bone structure. 'Don't you *dare* say anything about us to anyone,' she demanded fiercely, burrowing with some wildness into her huge black handbag, 'or you'll ruin everything.'

Arthur was speechless, gazing with spellbound horror at the sparkle on her visible and ungloved left hand. Was it conceivable that she had bought some trinket and was going about claiming a relationship between them?

'Because I'm getting married,' said Rosalinda rapidly. She had found what she was looking for and now slapped down on the nearest table a thick fold of what later turned out to be blank paper. 'I told Nicky I had to deliver some typing—you wouldn't believe how jealous he is—but I had to warn you, don't say a *word*. He'd kill us both.'

Arthur stared at her, stunned, realising in a grop-
ing fashion that it must be Nicky outside, that the
diamond was real and nothing to do with him, that
Rosalinda herself was now actually afraid of discovery. 'But . . . when we had lunch the other
day—'

'I didn't have this, then,' said Rosalinda, admir-
ing her ring. She added with a trace of mockery,
'Besides, I wanted to see what you'd do.'

In a very few words it became clear that Arthur
had been right in his suspicion: she had only drifted
into his orbit because of a gigantic quarrel with
Nicky, who had then taken himself off to San
Diego. Returning full of love and repentance, and
plainly imagining Rosalinda to be as mournful as he
during his absence, he must not be allowed under
any circumstances to suspect an involvement with
another man.

'He has a very hot temper,' said Rosalinda, glowing and obviously understating the case, 'so—'

'Wait,' said Arthur. Even in his astonishment he
had been conscious of a growing wrath at Lopez. 'I
don't think you know that your stepfather—'

Rosalinda, who had been moving restively towards the door, listened in turn. Her face grew
ferocious; she hissed something in Spanish, something she seldom did, and it did not sound fond.
Snatching a pen from her bag, seizing up a piece of
the blank paper she had flung down, she scribbled,
tore, and handed the paper to Arthur. She said
blackly, 'If he bothers you again, if he opens his
mouth, ask him about this licence number.'

That had been the strangeness in Lopez: a surreptitious haste because he was acting without his
stepdaughter's knowledge or consent, and had

reason to fear a reprisal. Was the licence plate number something to do with a stolen car? Rosalinda seemed very sure of its power, and Arthur did not ask but folded the slip of paper prudently into his wallet.

Should he, out of a vast relief Rosalinda could not even guess at, offer something in the way of a wedding present? Good God, no. Instead, a little stiffly, Arthur bestowed his felicitations, which Rosalinda received with open impatience and then was gone, out of his house, his driveway, and his life.

It would be hours before he grew aware that the buffer between him and the full realisation of the fact and the manner of Molly's dying was gone too.

The next day was one of the longest Eve had ever lived through.

In at least partial explanation of his unheralded attack of homesickness the night before, Ambrose had a sore throat and a temperature. ('You know, when I saw him out in his bare feet in the wet grass last week, I *thought* . . .' said Iris Saxon judicially, tying on her apron.)

At ten o'clock Ambrose was still gratified by breakfast in bed and other unusual attentions: this was more like it, his manner implied. By eleven he was growing querulous, by twelve he was huddled rebelliously before the television set in bathrobe and slippers. Iris Saxon cast him a disapproving look, and inquired of Eve in a low voice, 'Oughtn't he to be in bed?'

Was Celia often made to feel like this, the mistress of a misbehaving puppy at the obedience trials? 'Probably,' said Eve, and added with restraint, 'On the other hand, a doctor would want him dressed and driven sixteen miles to the Clinic, where we would wait forever without a scheduled appointment, so maybe . . .'

That was one facet of the day. Another was that Eve, a victim of her own impulsive tale about Ambrose's imminent departure, was forced to employ the time not spent at his beck and call in emptying bureau drawers and closets for every last stitch of his clothing. In this she was spurred on by Iris's memory: 'Didn't he have a blue sweater, hon? . . . I can only find one of these striped socks . . . This little shirt is perfectly good if you can find me two white buttons.'

The television set went tirelessly on, Ambrose croaked various demands, Eve toiled away in search of socks and buttons and was called back intermittently for a decision as to whether this or that garment was worth mending. At one point, feeling enormously guilty, she retreated into her bedroom and read the morning paper, turning the pages as noiselessly as a burglar.

In view of the lack of developments, it was not surprising that the Pulliam and Morley murders had been relegated to an inside page, under 'Continue Investigation in Valley Slayings' and 'Vandals Strike at Home of Victim's Husband.' What did surprise Eve was the curiously palliative tone that emanated from the front-page account of the suspect's apprehension in the candy-store affair. He had been in a Flagstaff jail when Molly Pulliam died, and yet in some manner what emerged from the careful, factual story was that three women had been killed within a short period of time and a fingerprint had finally been left behind. It created the kind of atmosphere in which even sensible people said, 'I don't care, there's something awfully fishy about it.'

Eve laid the paper down and gazed at the massed cottonwood leaves, now crisped and browning from the rapidly chilling nights, that still pressed against her window. Was it possible that the murder of the two sisters would ultimately remain unsolved? Yes; you had only to read any newspaper to know that it was eminently possible. Certainly the police inquiries in Colorado, where both Molly and Jennifer had grown up, seemed to have produced nothing.

. . . Colorado, and the school where a woman related to Richard Morley had sat down to write, but had not completed, a suicide note. Was Henry Conlon aware that this carefully guarded piece of information had been tossed casually to Nina Earl, and in turn to Eve?

He was, Eve found when he telephoned in mid-afternoon. He did not say in so many words that he had talked to Nina; he wanted to know, in a voice that sounded both tired and queerly relieved, if he could come by possibly as late as ten o'clock because there was an Advertising Awards dinner.

'Yes, I'll be up. I hope Cox-Ivanhoe wins a lot of awards.'

'Thank you,' said Henry bleakly. 'I suppose you know that Mrs Ivanhoe will be there, and I'll be in charge.'

Clara Ivanhoe, widow of the founding partner and a large shareholder in the firm, presented a problem in this annual affair which she insisted on attending. In her seventies, not certifiable but noticeably erratic, she sometimes got so carried away with indignation about awards to rival firms that she thumped her salad plate, with a resultant flying about of slippery greens, and on one terrible occasion she had risen to her feet to begin a denunciatory speech.

Someone always had to police her, and this year it was Henry. 'Good luck,' said Eve.

Ambrose was unmanned by fever and aspirin and slept peaceably, and the day finally ended. 'Thanks as usual, Iris, for repairing us again,' said Eve at five o'clock, the folded check already handed over. She was filled with sudden compunction at the older woman's drawn look: for the first time in their acquaintance, the wistful little girl inside seemed to have given up and died. 'You did much too much today. I never realised that Ambrose and I had so many hems and buttons between us. Things will be better next week, I promise.'

'Don't be silly. I don't know what I'd do without you, in more ways than one,' said Iris, her face lighting briefly. 'Say goodbye to the little boy for me, will you, as I probably won't see him again? I hope he'll be feeling better in the morning.'

'I'm sure he will be. I know he's had measles, so it isn't that, and it doesn't look like what I remember of mumps.'

They were both, by now, listening openly and vainly for the clatter of Ned Saxon's old car. 'I wonder if I'd better call?' said Iris presently, when the tall windows had turned a deep steel colour against the lamplight. 'That darned car—'

But Ned Saxon arrived while she was at the telephone. 'Sorry I'm late,' he said, smiling ruddily on the threshold and rubbing his gloved hands together. 'I had a little trouble getting started—I guess the old buggy's feeling the cold.' His mouth quirked at Eve. 'I have half a mind to turn it in and get a Cadillac.'

'That's a thought,' said Eve, smiling back, and Iris said with unaccustomed tartness, 'Don't let's stand here with the cold coming in, the little boy's sick. Did you ever find out what he was looking for, Eve—his racket, or whatever it was?'

It was by now a familiar contradiction in Iris that in spite or perhaps because of her lack of enthusiasm for Ambrose, she was scrupulously attentive to all details concerning him. 'Oh, his rockles,' said Eve. Aware of the prickly sensitivity of both the Saxons, she avoided looking at Ned. 'Yes, it turned out to be an old cloth with a coloured patch that he—lost somewhere.'

'Kids,' commented Ned with an indulgent chuckle. He was obviously feeling the chill in the dark-pearl air; his massive shoulders had moved in a quick shudder. He took his wife's arm protectively, and after a polite hope that Eve would not contract Ambrose's malady and a final 'See you next week' they were gone.

Eve brought Ambrose his dinner in bed and sat with him while he consumed it by infinitesimal degrees and only when reminded. His thoughts had reverted, but in a contended way, to the airplane under construction. Even when he inquired, 'Is it made yet?' he was not really impatient; he seemed, if anything, a little reluctant to relinquish this drama so soon. Eve assured him that the workers were keeping busy, left him with some marbles to pour noisily back and forth into two plastic cups, and prepared her own dinner.

Her inner flutteriness was, she informed herself,

purely a state of suspense over Jennifer Morley's involvement with the affair at the Lockwood School years ago; it had nothing to do with Henry Conlon himself. She had seen him two or three times since the afternoon when he had gazed at her with such total familiarity across the failing light in her living room, and each time they had been like two particles on a laboratory slide which, out of some imposed chemical reaction, move delicately about each other but never touch.

The trouble was that along with the new formality came a new awareness, all the stronger for being concealed. Which was natural enough, thought Eve. He had been through one disastrous experience with marriage, she had been through one disastrous engagement. Neither wanted to be involved so soon again, and both recognised the threat of involvement.

. . . The rattling of marbles slowed to a trickle and finally stopped. Eve tiptoed into Ambrose's room, removed the marbles and cups from his bed with infinite care, and switched off the light. It only occurred to her then that it had been a considerable time since she had closed the front door behind the Saxons, and that she had not bolted it.

She did that now and drew the curtains everywhere, but not with the urgency of a few nights ago. She was not foolish enough to think that the apprehension of a young panic-stricken killer had anything to do with the savagery that had invaded the Valley, but in some subtle way the pressure had relaxed.

The passage of time was reassuring in itself. Alone with a three-year-old child, Eve must have been vulnerable on countless occasions since hearing the click of the receiver in the Morley house. The very lack of any menace did not suggest to her a deliberate lulling, a false all-clear while an attack was being mounted.

Pushing aside a fold of toile, she saw that blackness had descended completely around the little house. Like Molly Pulliam, like Jennifer Morley, she was not, at this particular time, afraid.

CHAPTER
NINETEEN

. . . Had the child seen the shaft of the hammer in the twinkling before it was engulfed in the snatched-up rag—or seeing it, recognised it for what it was? And if he had, what was the word of a three-year-old? He couldn't read, obviously, and it was unlikely that anyone would have filled him in on the details of a woman bludgeoned to death with a hammer.

But he was a queer little kid, abnormal in Ned Saxon's cold judgment, and he had certainly told Eve Quinn at least some of the details of the incident of the tool shed, when he had fastened his attention on the cloth and wanted it back. 'You're not supposed to be in here at all, boy,' Ned had told him, 'and if you don't want the seat of your pants warmed you'll get out right now.'

'I want my rockles,' the child had said, scarlet and stubborn and frightened—at the threat of a spanking, Ned had thought at the time.

'Your what? Oh, this thing. Let me tell you, young fellow, you're lucky I found it, it's crawling with deadly germs. Tell you what, we'll leave it locked up in here and it'll die all by itself.' Ned had made a swift feinting throw with the rag, restored it to his pocket while the child was still staring round-eyed into a corner, bustled him out of the tool shed.

And the child had tumbled off in the sunlight with considerable speed. Ned knew from Iris of his preoccupation with germs; what he did not know was the peculiar horror of the other concept he had planted—the solitary sickening, and death in darkness, of a piece of cloth.

The cloth which was to shroud the hammer head from any traces that washing might miss.

Obviously Ambrose had not forgotten, and Eve Quinn, speaking of the incident tonight, had carefully averted her glance from Ned. Was she asking in her mind why a man who so conscientiously accounted for his every footstep on her property (and she had never guessed at the iron malice behind all that forelock-tugging) had made an independent visit to the tool shed? Would she ultimately connect that with the vain police search for the weapon that had killed Molly Pulliam?

No, because she would not be allowed the time.

In spite of his relatively short acquaintance with her, Ned Saxon hated Eve Quinn with all the ferocity of his hatred for the Pulliam and Morley women, with some added embellishments.

There was the galling matter of her youth—he guessed her, correctly, to be about twenty-five—while she was in a position to hand out work and careless checks to a woman old enough to be her grandmother.

There was the fact of her single state: in a region of severe economic stress, while older men like Ned Saxon haunted employment offices for jobs in order to support their wives, Eve Quinn had contrived a very good salary on the strength of her looks and the glib products of a typewriter.

And there was the child, whom *his wife* was expected to toady to and tidy up after, a boy who thought it entertaining, as an especially cruel taunt, to throw horned toads into Iris's lap. Even then, such were Eve Quinn's powers of deceit that Iris said thoughtfully, 'She doesn't seem to spank him very often, but somehow or other she's able to handle him . . .'

Now, driving to the supermarket as usual on this day of the week, Ned reflected that he had been given another omen in that parting exchange on Eve Quinn's doorstep. It was as if she had been delivered into his hands.

The Saxons had dinner early, as usual, and Iris forewent her frequent wry apology for their being so unfashionable. She seemed to have aged ten years in a few days, and Ned, washing and drying the dishes, saw superimposed on her strained face an image of Eve Quinn, young and erect, lamplight from the comfortable pretty room behind her fringing her fair hair with gold as she stood in the doorway . . .

A half carton of milk went crashing and spilling into the sink. Iris glanced, and said as though close to tears, 'Oh, *no*. That's the last of the milk.'

'I'll go get some, it won't take me ten minutes.' Ned hung up the dishtowel, rolled down his sleeves.

'We can do without it till morning,' said Iris— sternly, for her, because it was Ned who occasionally woke in the night and could only calm his stomach with milk. 'We have some soda crackers.'

'Nonsense.' Ned was by now into his half-respectable topcoat, which had last been aired at Jennifer Morley's funeral. 'Damp out tonight, I really feel the cold,' he explained, taking the car keys from his customary old jacket.

'I don't think you should go out,' said Iris with a peculiar fixity. 'I really don't, Ned. You had trouble with the car, coming to get me—'

'The engine was just cold,' said Ned, who had had no trouble at all; a terrible suspicion that had flashed all through him ebbed comfortably away. 'I'll give it a try, and if it doesn't start up at once I won't go.'

Iris heard the stumble and catch of the motor, the rattle of the car as it moved away. She put her flattened hands hard against her cheeks, staring at nothing, and presently, like a woman under hypnosis, she walked to the telephone and dialed.

'Eve? Sorry to bother you, and you'll think I'm an idiot, but we passed a couple of police cars with their lights flashing in your area, and I wondered if—you know, you're all locked and bolted and so on.'

'Yes, I am,' said Eve Quinn's voice, 'as of a few minutes ago, but thanks for reminding me.'

'What I'd do, and what Ned advises,' said Iris, her tone sharpening, 'is turn off maybe a few of your lights—after all, you're known to be alone there—and don't open the door tonight to *anyone*. I mean that, Eve, because it gave me the funniest feeling, seeing those police cars . . .'

Ned Saxon walked briskly away from his car, its hood up and illuminated by a street light, familiar to most of the people in this neighbourhood. Three blocks south, on one of the main streets, he entered a used-car lot.

He had been here yesterday, wearing a soft hat, as he did tonight, which did not entirely conceal his hair but made it less noticeable. He had inspected a modest dark blue Ford with lukewarm interest and the disparaging comment that he could get a comparable model for forty dollars less at—

Here he had produced his wallet and opened it in apparent search for a notation. The bills from Molly Pulliam's purse, exhumed from the chair with the broken spring and converted into ones except for a ten allowed to show its corner, made a respectable bulge. The salesman grew more affable at once, whisking the door open with an unabashed flourish on an interior which had been ill-treated. Would Mr Turner care to take the Ford out for a run?

Ned Saxon had said that he hadn't time this afternoon but might very well be back with his sister, for whom the car was intended. He departed with the conviction that here, if he should want it in the next few days, was free anonymous transportation while his own car was visibly elsewhere.

Business was brisker tonight at the used-car lot; the salesman greeted Ned as Mr Turner, handed over the keys to the Ford, and hastened back to a couple interested in a station wagon. Three minutes after that Ned was in the little market where they occasionally bought emergency items; having borrowed the phone he told Iris ruefully that he should have taken her advice about the car. 'It's at the corner of Melrose and Sixth. I'll have another try at it and then see if I can get someone to give me a push—if I leave it there all night there won't be a single tyre on it by morning. I just didn't want you to worry.'

The young clerk at the counter rang up the sale of a quart of milk and shook his head in sympathy. 'They could carry away the chassis they'd do it, some of these kids around here,' he said, and then, 'Getting real cold out, I hear.'

Ned made a mock gesture of wiping his forehead. 'Maybe if you're not hiking it is.' He felt so elated at the smooth running of things, and so drawn to this spotty lad who could bear out his story in the unlikely event that it ever needed bearing out, that he was actually reluctant to leave. But once he was in the Ford again, the dark, modest, secret-keeping Ford, he had to watch his speed.

Improvisation was best; he knew that now with the absolute and dazzled certainty of a novice gambler. His watch, held briefly close to the dashboard, said eight twenty-five.

Eve came away from the telephone faintly, unfairly indignant at Iris Saxon. The other woman was only being kind and overanxious, as usual, but to someone alone with a sick child the well-meant warning had the effect of a stone flung shatteringly into a pond which had just managed to piece its reflections together again.

It should have been just the opposite—surely patrol cars made a reassuring presence—but it was not. Eve found herself listening edgily to a stillness which now, thanks to Iris, seemed false instead of tranquil.

Even Ambrose, sleeping snorelessly, seemed part of the conspiracy. What was called for here was either an extremely good book or something really engrossing on television. It was far too early to expect Henry Conlon; although Eve had never been to the awards dinner, she suspected that the speeches were barely under way. And it was not a function from which Henry could slip unobtrusively away; he had to keep an eye on aberrant Mrs Ivanhoe.

For reasons which she would not have dreamed of divulging openly to herself, reasons connected with a cunning mask of sound, Eve did not go near the television set. Instead, although she knew from past rereadings that the only pleasant character in it was shortly to be felled by an elm tree, she picked up her English novel and settled herself in a corner of the couch.

Instantly, as though she had been watched and patiently waited for to do just this, there was an echoing thud from outside.

Eve was violently on her feet, frozen there with her book in an iron grip so as not to betray her position by so much as the whisper of a page. In one compartment of her mind she was trying to assure her own panicked senses that the thud had been an impersonal accident and was nothing to do with her; in another she thought wildly, If it happens again I'll call the Sheriff. (And tell him what? That I hear noises outside? And even if they come, which they probably won't, how long—?)

There seemed to be no passage of time involved in this voiceless discussion, only Eve's dangerously heavy heartbeats before she recognised a new sound, this one brisk, open, announcing itself clearly as someone approaching her door and knocking. 'Miss Quinn? It's me—Ned Saxon.'

Eve drew in her breath with a tremble of relief, took two steps towards the door, checked herself. Ned Saxon—or someone imitating his voice, someone who knew she would trust him? Jennifer Morley had opened her door without fear, and never reentered it again. She stood paralysed, still gripping her book as though it represented safety, aware that to be *known* to be at bay was perhaps the most perilous thing of all.

The knock was repeated. The familiar voice said with sharpness, 'Miss Quinn? Everything all right in there?'

It was unmistakably Iris's husband—no tongue, however malevolent, could be that clever—and Eve called, 'Yes, I'm coming,' while she slid back the bolt and twisted the lock and switched on the outside light. Even then she felt a last-minute twinge of fear (this is what idiots do) but when she had the door open it really was Ned Saxon, the radiance showering down on his creamy-orange head.

CHAPTER
TWENTY

He was holding out her driving gloves, smiling apologetically but at the same time glancing curiously into the room behind her as if he wondered why, fully dressed as she was, she had been so long in answering his knock. He said, 'Sorry to bother you, but Iris got these mixed up with hers by mistake and thought you'd be wanting them tomorrow.'

'Oh, thanks very much. You shouldn't have gone to all that trouble, but I can't tell you how glad I am to see you,' said Eve in a tumble, taking the gloves without a glance. 'I heard the funniest sound outside, and I suppose I was nervous after Iris telephoned, and I was imagining all kinds of things.'

Ned Saxon swung sharply away from her and started out into the dark. Even his back looked furiously alert. Eve went on, voluble in her own release from tension, 'It's nice to know you met two police cars in this area, but it would be even nicer to know they weren't needed.'

The blue gaze returned to her face, looking blind—but that was reaction to the light. Then, 'Yes,' said Ned with sudden briskness . . . 'If you have a flashlight I'll just take a look around for you while I'm here.'

His very bulk was reassuring, Eve thought, watching him move away behind the carving gold. She was already beginning to feel a little embar-

rassed at her own extreme reaction to what had
been in all probability a stone sailed idly over the
wall; there were people to whom walls presented an
automatic challenge. Still, it was pleasant to know
that Ned Saxon was out there, even—on the still air
she heard the click of the padlock—checking the
tool shed.

It seemed thankless to close the door entirely in
spite of the penetrating cold. Eve left it a few inches
open and was in her bedroom collecting a sweater
when Ned Saxon's call reached her: 'Miss Quinn?
Better come out and see what they've done to your
car.'

What they've done—it sounded far more frightening than any amount of mere mechanical
damage. Eve snatched up her coat instead, ran out
into the guiding path of the flashlight slanting
through the open gate. This was no casual malice;
someone had meant to immobilise her tonight, and
it was only the merest chance, through the accident
of a pair of gloves, that there was another car here,
to take her and Ambrose—

But there wasn't another car. Eve's stood alone
in the driveway. Then how had Ned Saxon . . . ?

Her feet were still carrying her mechanically
around the hood of the car, apparently undamaged
on the near side; her brain, because of her bewilderment, made much slower progress. It informed her only now that, straining as she had been
for any sound after that earthy thud, she had heard
nothing until, a few seconds later, Ned's brisk
approach by foot. How odd that he hadn't heard
the sound too, in the total stillness of the night.

How much odder that Iris, saying with such in-
tensity, 'Don't open the door to *anyone*,' should

not have added, 'except Ned, he's on his way with your gloves.'

Which Eve could have sworn she had left on the front seat of her car.

Late, too late, she glanced incredulously up from her right front tyre at the face lit from below, and saw what Molly Pulliam and Jennifer Morley had seen in the last seconds before they died.

She thought at first that the blinding light was an explosion of pain inside her head from the glancing blow he had struck her with some heavy metal object—glancing because she had had that infinitesimal warning. But the light was accompanied by an enormous heavy roar that drowned out the voice full of loathing and unimaginable invective, threaded through with, 'All the same, every one of you, all the same,' while her face ground with bleeding impact into dirt and stones.

In absolute terror, mindlessly abject with pain, she had a brief delirious dream of Henry Conlon's shoes, and a strange dream about her cousin Celia's husband, whose name escaped her. 'Take care of her,' a voice said—well, someone should. She turned her head querulously on the dirt and stones, and gazed at the dizzying perforations of a sound-proofed hospital ceiling.

In the day and a half lost forever out of her life, Eve said tremblingly at some point, 'I can't—I don't . . .' and there was a soothing professional voice there at once. 'Yes, you can, Miss Quinn. Now give me your right hand . . . now your left. There, you see?'

They had no notion of what she meant, and with

severe concussion and seventeen stitches taken in the right side of her head Eve could not explain the special horror of such hatred and purpose in another human face. Was it possible ever again to trust a casual connection to whom she had been unaware of doing harm? How, in the future, survive in any kind of personal world?

Nina Earl sent flowers, and Cox-Ivanhoe came up handsomely with dark red roses. Henry Conlon, who had flickered unevenly in and out of Eve's consciousness, brought Scotch, and said, 'Don't worry, I asked your doctor and he said it was perfectly all right. I'm not likely to want to do away with you at this stage.'

This stage? Eve turned her head dizzily, caught a tag end of memory, said, 'If you came to tell me . . . I don't have to know, really. I'd rather not.'

'That was the mistake Jennifer made,' said Henry with force, and told her.

It was all so simple—but so was a grain of sand that occasionally ended up in an astonishing growth, or a harmless snowball which, unimpeded, could grow to crushing proportions. It had its beginnings in a practical joke played by the then Molly Vane, aged seventeen, on a vindictive and neurotic housemother at the Lockwood School.

He gathered, said Henry, that Mrs Marguerite Sellers ought never to have held that position at a girls' school; she was, to put it at its simplest, jealous of her pretty and carefree charges. She had been especially harsh with Molly, who had retaliated with the inventive but innocent cruelty of her age by arranging to have an older friend, handsome in his Air Force uniform, take Mrs Sellers to an inn on the pretext of wishing to enroll his younger sister in the school, ply her with flattery and stunning amounts of sherry, and return her to the dormitory thoroughly, maudlinly drunk.

It was Easter vacation and the school was almost empty, but Mrs Sellers' imagination must have peopled it with laughing, ridiculing faces. At any rate, three days later she had done what had in all probability been at the back of her mind for some time—and she had written a note blaming Molly Vane.

Jennifer, who was working in the office to help with Molly's fees, was horrified when she found out, belatedly, what her sister had done. She had gone to apologise, and found the dead woman and the indictment of Molly. Instinctively, because it seemed monstrous that the death of an emotionally unstable person should be placed at the door of a young girl who had intended only mischief, she destroyed the note. Then, frantic with worry about the possible consequences of her own action, she told Henry Conlon, whom she had known all her life, and no one else.

Mrs Sellers' only relative, a much younger and distant cousin named Richard Morley, turned up to make the funeral arrangements. By the time when the attraction between him and Jennifer Vane was absolute, it was much too late to say, 'Oh, by the way, your cousin blamed my sister for her suicide, but I tore up the note . . .' It grew more impossible with every passing year; Richard Morley, tense, possessive, would argue to himself, not illogically, 'If she could have kept this from me, what else has she concealed?'

It was the newspaper coverage of Molly's murder which brought the typed and anonymous note that had sent Jennifer into a panic. It said, 'Maybe someone else knew the truth about Marguerite Sellers.'

'The door of the woman's room was unlocked,' said Henry, getting up to peer out at the hospital's deserted sun deck, 'and Jennifer always knew it was a possibility that another person had read the note before she did and kept quiet about it simply in order not to get involved. Well, somebody obviously had, and for the whole business to come out now—Molly's trick in the first place, Jennifer's destroying the evidence, Jennifer married to the cousin . . .' He gave Eve a straight clear glance. 'She'd gone to such pains about keeping it quiet that it was like an orphan child handed on. I felt—responsible.'

'So you were off finding out who—'

'Yes, and it wasn't hard at all except that Jennifer could hardly have undertaken it. After we eliminated you,' said Henry, smiling wryly down at Eve, 'Jennifer remembered a girl in Molly's dormitory who just might have had a younger sister visiting— that was allowed over vacation. And she did, and I found her, and she hadn't meant the note as a threat at all but as a possible help. She didn't sign her name because her husband is an extremely important figure in Albuquerque and she's currently a voluntary patient at a very nice plush place for alcoholics. They have children. I couldn't see,' said Henry, 'that bringing all this to light would do anybody any good. But I had to make sure there was no connection . . .'

A nurse came in with a pill for Eve, smiled at Henry, and left. Better get it over with, thought Eve, drowsy even before the medication. She still couldn't move her head with any suddenness, but she glanced obliquely at the morning newspaper; the evening paper had not yet come. 'Is Ned Saxon—?'

She knew most of it by now: that Clara Ivanhoe, problematical as never before, had had to be escorted away from the awards dinner very early by Henry; that Henry's headlights had come wheeling onto the scene of Eve's apparently dead face being slammed into the ground by Ned Saxon; that Saxon had fled to what turned out to be a car from a used-car lot and driven it with tremendous force, and certain intent, into a huge cottonwood at what was known appropriately as Dead Man's Corner. Somehow, until this morning, he had survived a depressed fracture of the skull and other injuries.

'He died this afternoon,' said Henry, voice quiet and face hard. 'His wife won't admit that she suspected him, but I think she must have, and for heaven's sake don't worry about *her*, something can be done . . .'

How many enemies were there, really; how many private executioners of people who did not even know that they had transgressed? On the other hand, how many people like Henry, as safe as a vault, as thoughtful of the reputation of a woman seeking help? There was probably a balance on the right side, there must be . . .

'You're asleep,' said Henry's voice from a great distance.

'No, I'm not. I was just thinking—don't go away yet, because I was just . . .' mumbled Eve, and was kissed, very gently, and slept.

OUR RECORD
OF PREVIOUS CRIMES

Some of the exciting tales of murder, mystery, danger, detection and suspense already published in Keyhole Crime.

 Keyhole Crime

OUR RECORD
OF PREVIOUS CRIMES

Some of the exciting tales of murder, mystery, danger, detection and suspense already published in Keyhole Crime.

Keyhole Crime

A FEW CLUES ABOUT MORE GREAT TITLES YOU'LL SOON BE SEEING IN KEYHOLE CRIME

STAR TRAP
Simon Brett

The star is Christopher Milton in the lead part of a new musical. The trap is a door through which Charles Paris falls accidentally. Or was it an accident? Then the rehearsal pianist is shot in the hand by an airgun pellet and one of the actors tumbles down some stairs and breaks his leg. Or was he pushed? Charles Paris, actor/amateur detective saves the show and reveals the saboteur with a mixture of luck, experience and sheer talent.

THE BEAUTIFUL GOLDEN FRAME
Peter Chambers

Millionaire Bernard Rivers hired Private Eye, Mark Preston when a madwoman threatened to burn down his home. Rivers didn't care about his house but he did care about the picture inside, for it was the sole reminder of his beautiful wife Judith, killed two years before. After her death, Rivers framed her picture in solid gold and hid it away behind electrically controlled shutters for his eyes only. And Preston knew that stopping a mad aggressor with a flaming torch was almost impossible.

 Keyhole Crime

A FEW CLUES ABOUT MORE GREAT TITLES YOU'LL SOON BE SEEING IN KEYHOLE CRIME

STAR TRAP
Simon Brett

The star is Christopher Milton in the lead part of a new musical. The trap is a door through which Charles Paris falls accidentally. Or was it an accident? Then the rehearsal pianist is shot in the hand by an airgun pellet and one of the actors tumbles down some stairs and breaks his leg. Or was he pushed? Charles Paris, actor/amateur detective saves the show and reveals the saboteur with a mixture of luck, experience and sheer talent.

THE BEAUTIFUL GOLDEN FRAME
Peter Chambers

Millionaire Bernard Rivers hired Private Eye, Mark Preston when a madwoman threatened to burn down his home. Rivers didn't care about his house but he did care about the picture inside, for it was the sole reminder of his beautiful wife Judith, killed two years before. After her death, Rivers framed her picture in solid gold and hid it away behind electrically controlled shutters for his eyes only. And Preston knew that stopping a mad aggressor with a flaming torch was almost impossible.

 Keyhole Crime

A FEW CLUES ABOUT MORE GREAT TITLES YOU'LL SOON BE SEEING IN KEYHOLE CRIME

THE FAMILY VAULT
Charlotte MacLeod

When her Great Uncle Frederick dies and the family vault is opened to receive his body, Sarah Kelling peers inside and sees a skull with blood-coloured rubies winking amongst its grinning teeth. Had the flamboyant nightclub queen, Ruby Redd who disappeared thirty years before, been buried alive in their vault? Who could have buried her there and why?

EXTRA KILL
Dell Shannon

The young cop was sure his short Los Angeles career was to come to an abrupt end when he gave a speeding ticket to Lieutenant Luis Mendoza of the Homicide Division. But at least the mistake enabled him to take a disregarded piece of evidence about a recent off-licence shoot-out directly to Mendoza himself. The Lieutenant asked his colleagues to rake over the meagre facts again and uncovered the theft of $2,300 and a bizarre double murder.

Look out for them wherever you normally buy paperbacks

 Keyhole Crime

If you have any difficulty obtaining any of these titles, or if you would like further information on forthcoming titles in Keyhole Crime please write to:-
Keyhole Crime, PO Box 236, Thornton Road, Croydon, Surrey CR9 3RU.